She knew what was happ—
his arms…their lips were

He was kissing her and she was

God help her, but she loved bein

Though she should stop it, she couldn't. She didn't want to stop it.

She wanted to savor this moment. To take it with her when they went their separate ways.

It doesn't have to be separate ways.

"I'm sorry," he whispered breathlessly against her neck. "I shouldn't."

"No, you should." She kissed him again. "There don't have to be promises, George. Let's just have this time and see what happens."

"Samantha, if you touch me again…if you look at me a certain way…I may forget that we aren't together. I may forget that we're only supposed to be friends."

"So then forget that." She kissed him. "Give me this. Please."

He'd come to her door tonight. He'd opened up. And maybe nothing would continue once they got up north, but she couldn't resist him.

The kiss deepened, his tongue melding with hers, his hands in her hair as he pressed her against her couch, his hands traveling up and down her body, chest to chest, but not skin to skin, which was what she wanted.

Samantha grinned as he scooped her up, holding her in his strong arms.

If she didn't do this, she'd regret it.

And she was tired of living with regrets.

Dear Reader

Thank you for picking up a copy of DARE SHE DATE AGAIN?

You might recognise the hero, George Atavik, from my debut Mills & Boon® Medical Romance™, SAFE IN HIS HANDS.

George was such a charming, interesting character. I knew from the very first moment he walked onto the page in my first book, spouting nonsense about his love of Westerns and his love of planes, that he would have to have his own book.

Of course I wasn't going to make it easy for George. He had to work hard for his story, and for the heroine Samantha—but then love is never easy, even after it's won.

I love stories of second chances, even if that second chance is with someone different. Sometimes love ends too quickly when our loved one is taken from us, either through death or drifting apart. Still, love always seems to find a way.

I hope you enjoy DARE SHE DATE AGAIN?, and I hope I've done justice to George's story.

I love hearing from readers, so please drop by my website, www.amyruttan.com, or give me a shout on Twitter @ruttanamy.

With warmest wishes

Amy Ruttan

DARE SHE DATE AGAIN?

BY
AMY RUTTAN

First published in Great Britain 2014
by Mills & Boon, an imprint of Harlequin (UK) Limited,
Large Print edition 2015
Eton House, 18-24 Paradise Road,
Richmond, Surrey, TW9 1SR

© 2014 Amy Ruttan

ISBN: 978-0-263-25472-3

Harlequin (UK) Limited's policy is to use papers that are natural, renewable and recyclable products and made from wood grown in sustainable forests. The logging and manufacturing processes conform to the legal environmental regulations of the country of origin.

Printed and bound in Great Britain
by CPI Antony Rowe, Chippenham, Wiltshire

Born and raised on the outskirts of Toronto, Ontario, **Amy Ruttan** fled the big city to settle down with the country boy of her dreams. When she's not furiously typing away at her computer she's mom to three wonderful children, who have given her another job as a taxi driver.

A voracious reader, she was given her first romance novel by her grandmother, who shared her penchant for a hot romance. From that moment Amy was hooked by the magical worlds, handsome heroes and sigh-worthy romances contained in the pages, and she knew what she wanted to be when she grew up.

Life got in the way, but after the birth of her second child she decided to pursue her dream of becoming a romance author.

Amy loves to hear from readers. It makes her day, in fact. You can find out more about Amy at her website: www.amyruttan.com

Recent titles by Amy Ruttan:

PREGNANT WITH THE SOLDIER'S SON
MELTING THE ICE QUEEN'S HEART
SAFE IN HIS HANDS

These books are also available in eBook format from www.millsandboon.co.uk

Dedication

This book is dedicated to my editor,
Laura McCallen, who believed in this book and
who believes in me. Thank you for all you do.

CHAPTER ONE

JUST ONE MORE training session.

Another two months. That was it.

Samantha Doxtator took a deep breath and looked at the roster. She only had to mentor one more paramedic in training and she could leave her Health Air training job behind and move on to their air program in Thunder Bay.

Thunder Bay was her dream. She'd bought a house there. She'd finally give her son the life he deserved and best of all she'd be in the air, saving lives.

She walked over to where the dispatcher, Lizzie Bathurst, was handing out the prospective paramedics' files to their mentors.

"Morning, Lizzie."

Lizzie didn't say anything, but that wasn't unusual for her.

"So who am I mentoring for this *last* session?"

Samantha asked eagerly, putting the emphasis on the word "last" as she clapped her hands and rubbed them together.

She was so ready to move up to Thunder Bay now. Most of her family had relocated up there when her father had died. In the north, her son Adam could grow up with cousins. He'd have a yard to play in instead of a patio off a ground-floor apartment.

Adam would be able to run and play outside, like she had been able to do when she'd been a kid growing up out in the country.

Adam may not have his dad any more, but he'd have a great, love-filled childhood. Thunder Bay had been her and her late husband's dream since they'd started training to become paramedics fourteen years ago.

It had just taken her a lot longer as her training had been sidetracked when Adam had been born and then Cameron had died.

Don't think about that.

Though she missed Cameron, he'd been gone

for some time. She usually welcomed him into her thoughts, but not today.

Today she had a job to do and she was going to complete it perfectly, so that her credentials would shine.

Work and giving it her all was how she'd managed to get through the years since Cameron had died. She didn't know any other way, or at least couldn't remember.

Samantha forced a smile again, trying to think about the positive. In a couple of months she'd be piloting a plane.

"Who will be my last, glorious graduate?" she asked.

Lizzie looked down her nose through her half-moon glasses. "'Glorious graduate'?"

Samantha frowned. "You're giving me a tough one, aren't you?"

Lizzie grinned. "You're the best. You can crack the hard nuts." She handed Samantha the file, which Samantha took with trepidation. She flipped it open to read the information.

"George Atavik. Wow, he's a long way from

home." Samantha was impressed. They hadn't had anyone from so far north come down this far south to take this program. "Wait, this says he's a pilot, with a heck of a lot of air time, but he wants to work in an ambulance?"

"I told you. A hard nut. He's got an impressive résumé and I want him in the air. You need to convince him to take Health Land and Air's training to become a pilot with them. I hate seeing talent go to waste."

Samantha worried her bottom lip. *Drat.* Why couldn't her last student be an easy one? Then again, she'd never been given the "easy" ones and she couldn't help but wonder if there was some kind of conspiracy against her.

"Hey, you're not sticking him with me because of our shared heritage, are you?" Samantha teased.

Lizzie's gaze narrowed. "Don't play that with me. You just want someone else."

Samantha chuckled. "Okay, you got me."

"You're the best, Samantha. You have the most experience working in ambulances."

"You're just buttering me up now. You're never this nice."

Lizzie grinned, one of those evil grins, and then it disappeared. "I don't know why he won't fly."

Samantha glanced at his file. "Maybe he wants to diversify. There aren't many ambulances up in Nunavut."

"Health Land and Air would like him to pilot, but if you can't convince him, we'll take him any way we can get him. Thunder Bay is short on ambulance operators so when he gets there at the end of the course he'll be snapped right up. By the way, you're working solo on this too."

"Solo?" Samantha asked. Now she really was shocked. "Usually we work in threes."

"Usually, but George Atavik has experience and he doesn't need the extra attention. Besides, as I said, you're the best."

Samantha nodded. "All right. I'll try."

"Don't try. Do. Now, go out there and meet him. The new recruits are meeting their mentors now."

Samantha tucked the file under her arm and headed into the other room, where about ten new recruits for the advance care program were arriving and their mentors were meeting them.

She spotted him from across the room. Well, the back of him as he was the only recruit standing by himself. The only one who looked completely at ease and didn't seem to be giving off a nervous energy.

"Atavik, George," she called out.

He turned around and she had to take a step back to catch her breath. His copper skin was flawless. He stood there dumbstruck at first as they surveyed each other, but then he smiled, and two deep dimples appeared, accentuating his brilliant white teeth.

His dark eyes twinkled like he held a mischievous secret, one that would take some coaxing to pry from him. His short black hair was tousled up in a faux hawk. He was tall, muscular but not bulky, lean. He was in good shape and the white crisp shirt and navy blue pants of a paramedic suited him well. Samantha hoped she wasn't staring at him with a gaping mouth.

It'd been some time since she'd appreciated a good-looking man. A really long time. Being a single mother didn't leave much opportunity to date.

He walked over to her, since she hadn't uttered a word since she'd called his name, and stuck out his hand. "I'm George Atavik."

Samantha licked her lips and stuck the file under her arm again to take his hand. Clumsily. "I'm Doxtator...Samantha. I'm Samantha Doxtator."

"Nice to meet you." He was polite and reserved.

Good. Maybe he wouldn't be as difficult as she'd originally thought.

Say something. You're just staring at him.

"Are we going to get started?" he asked, looking at her like she'd lost her mind.

Samantha cleared her throat. "Sorry, it's been a crazy day."

George nodded. "I take it you're one of the mentors I'm assigned to work with?"

"Yes, I'm your mentor. Your only mentor."

He looked around. "How come the others have two mentors?"

"You have more experience." Samantha cleared her throat and opened his file. "So we're going to be working together over the course of eight weeks while you get your advanced care paramedic training. Of course, with a pilot license, in less time you could get your critical care training—"

"I'm not interested." Suddenly the sparkle was gone from his eyes and the smile wiped away.

"Why not? You have a pilot—"

"I'm not interested. I'm here to work in an ambulance." He crossed his arms and Samantha got the hint not to push him any further.

"Okay. That's fine." Samantha pulled out some papers. "Just read these release waivers through, fill them out and we'll hit the road for your first day."

George nodded and she handed him the papers

and a pen. He took a seat at a nearby table and got straight to work on filling out the forms. Samantha moved away to give him some privacy.

As she went to get a cup of coffee she snuck a glance at him.

She wondered what made a pilot with so much air time give up flying. He had more air time than she did and she couldn't even imagine giving up flying.

So what drove him to ground himself, as it were?

As if he knew she was watching him, he looked up and their gazes locked across the room. His eyes were intense and pinned her to the spot. '

She turned away quickly, pretending to ignore him, only she could feel his eyes boring into the back of her neck. Like his eyes had leapt from his body and were drilling through her flesh. Heat bloomed in her cheeks and she wished her hair wasn't pulled back in a ponytail. Maybe then her long hair would hide the inevitable blush she knew was creeping up her neck into her cheeks.

Her late husband Cameron had thought her blushing was cute. It was something she couldn't control and she thought it was damn annoying. Control and order was everything to her.

When she glanced at him again, he had gone to his paperwork. He was so serious and focused. She respected it.

She had to get a grip on herself. She was his mentor, his teacher. It was her job to take him out and get a medic who was used to flying used to paramedic work in an ambulance instead.

Maybe a few times jostling in the back of an ambulance would change his tune.

Where he was from there weren't many roads. Only airplanes and snowmobiles or ATVs, apparently, if you wanted to get from town to town. Not like here.

She grinned a secret smile to herself and set her coffee cup down.

She'd have to test out his driving abilities at some point. Whether he could handle an ambulance or not would determine his future being a rig driver, and maybe if he didn't like it he would switch to air.

Not that she was going to sabotage him, but she was positive that someone not used to traffic would not enjoying driving an ambulance. It was only a matter of time before he was in the air again.

"Look alive, Atavik!"

"What?" George asked as he glanced up at Samantha. "What did you say?"

He was having a hard time focusing. He wasn't expecting his mentor to be one foxy-looking lady.

Foxy, George? Really? He fought the urge to groan in frustration with himself.

He wasn't sure what he'd been expecting when he'd arrived at the Health Land and Air training base in London, Ontario. It was sort of a mixer and meet-your-mentor kind of affair and then down to work. The other mentors were men. Big, beefy guys, and that's who George had been expecting to be his mentor.

He hadn't expected a gorgeous woman like Samantha Doxtator.

The idea of being here was to get away from women. Focus on his career, be the best paramedic he could be. Bring back the joy to his job by trying something new and different. He didn't want any distractions from that.

Distractions like this vixen.

She was tall, slim, but with curves in all the right places. George didn't like them thin as rails. It took all his willpower not to cock his head and check her out in her tight paramedic uniform.

Her ebony hair shone with purple undertones and was pulled back in a high ponytail, and she had olive-colored skin and almond-shaped eyes, which were the bluest he'd ever seen.

She was graceful, poised and also had a rod rammed up her backside.

Why was he always attracted to type-A women?

It was his curse.

Maybe because he'd grown up with so many type-A women. His sisters were workaholics, though Mentlana straddled types A and B. She was more type A when it came to his nephew Charlie's schedule.

No one messed with nap time.

His girlfriend in college had been a total type A and underneath that coiled, rigid exterior had been hot, explosive passion.

Too bad she'd decided that career and life in Toronto was more important to her than him.

Oh, well. He hadn't been too crushed when it had ended. It had been his last girlfriend who had crushed him. The woman he'd planned to marry. The woman who'd torn his heart in half, leaving his soul as battered and bruised as the outside of him was.

He wouldn't think of Cheryl. He wouldn't think of the one woman he ever thought of settling down with. The woman who was set to become his air paramedic partner once Ambrose moved away.

Thinking about Cheryl just reminded him why he didn't fly any longer and why he'd sworn off women and relationships completely. And he especially didn't want a relationship with another paramedic. The last time he'd done that, it hadn't worked out well at all.

"Mayday. Mayday. Mayday. Iqaluit Centre. This is Medic Air 1254. We have engine failure. I repeat, engine failure. We are making a forced landing twenty kilometers north. Four thousand feet descending, heading one-eighty."

Beads of sweat broke across his brow.

"Atavik, seriously, you look like you're going to be sick." Samantha was shaking her head.

George gave her a half-smile. "Sorry." He stacked his papers and stood up, placing them in Samantha's outstretched hand.

"You okay there?"

"Fine."

"Are you sure? I don't want you throwing up in here."

"I'm fine. Really," he snapped. He didn't need

her concern and he didn't want it. He was here to do a job.

Samantha cocked a finely arched brow. He knew she didn't believe him. "Okay. Then let's hit the road. Are you ready for that?"

Only he wasn't. He glanced covetously at the other trainees who had two mentors. Mentors who were male and were no temptation for him whatsoever. If there was someone else in the ambulance with them, then that person would be a buffer.

He didn't want to be tempted. He had to get a hold on this.

"So, are you ready?" Samantha asked again.

"Totally."

"Great!"

She looked a little gleeful about the prospect of taking him out. Oh, God. What did she have planned?

"Well, let me just file this away and we'll head out." She disappeared into an office and returned a minute later. "We're going to be riding in ambulance seven."

"Is it a good ambulance?" he asked, following her out to the garage.

George seriously doubted it, just by her eagerness.

She grinned. "You'll see."

"You're out to torture me, aren't you?" he mumbled under his breath, but she heard it because she was opening her mouth to say something when the ambulance beside the one they were heading for lit up, sirens blaring.

"Yo, shake a leg. There's a pile-up on Highway 401," someone shouted over the din.

"Come on, newbie." Samantha jogged toward the ambulance. "Time to see what you're made of."

George swallowed the anxious lump in his throat and followed Samantha into the front of the ambulance. When the doors were shut she started the engine and they headed out of the garage at breakneck speed.

"Flip that switch for me," she said, pointing to a red switch on the dash.

George flipped it up and the lights and sirens came on.

It was pretty awesome. His plane didn't have a siren or lights.

"You okay, Atavik?" Samantha asked again, shouting over the sirens.

"Fine."

Which was a lie.

He'd totally zoned out. He wasn't sure if it was the rocking motion of the ambulance as they raced along the road to the crash scene or if it was the fact he was a bit nervous about what a pile-up would bring.

He'd never been in the thick of it. There weren't large traffic accidents in Nunavut.

When he'd first come south the four hundred series of highways had been intimidating to him. In fact, London on the whole was a bit scary, though Charlotte's husband Quinn had got him situated and settled when he'd arrived.

George knew how to drive. He just preferred back roads. Although Quinn had eased him into city life and driving regularly, highways were still sketchy.

The blare of the siren made his ears hurt. He wasn't used to the sound. He didn't know if he'd ever get used to the sounds of the city. Especially riding in the front of an ambulance racing through city streets.

His plane had been silent.

Until it hadn't been.

Don't think about it.

George gave his best grin to Samantha and swiped the back of his arm across his forehead to mop up the sweat.

"Are you really okay?" she asked. "I don't want you to get sick on your first day."

"It's nothing."

"Hopefully not my driving?"

Yes, you're a menace, he wanted to say. To tease her. But he restrained himself.

"I'm fine," he snapped, and then immediately regretted sniping at her.

"Arrival on scene in five minutes. Pretty big pile-up on the 401."

George took a calming breath.

You've done this before. Countless times. Even if not on a grand scale like this.

Still, the idea of being a paramedic in a big city made him nervous. But he couldn't go back to Cape Recluse. After the crash the army had opened a base there, thus setting up a permanent air ambulance flight through Health Air.

His job was redundant.

Was he stupid to come down to southern Ontario and try something as alien to him as being a paramedic in heavy city traffic? Could he really still cling to his dream of saving lives if he couldn't fly?

He was older than the other students.

He was thirty-three.

What am I doing?

He was hoping that receiving this training would help him find the passion for saving lives again. That rush he used to feel before his accident.

Now he just went through the motions. It was

an act that he did well, but he longed for that rush again.

The ambulance slowed and George craned his neck as they came slowly down the off-ramp onto the highway.

He could see the smoke rising from the wreckage. There were police cars with their lights flashing and firefighters already on the scene, and when George looked behind them he could see other ambulances barreling down the off-ramp and more coming off further down the highway.

"You ready, Atavik?" She reached over and touched his knee, giving it a squeeze and also sending a jolt of pure electricity through him. He liked her touching him, and he didn't like that. He wanted to like it, but it was wrong.

"Ready."

Samantha pulled the ambulance over. "Show time!"

She gave him an encouraging smile as she got out of the ambulance.

George leapt down from the passenger side

and surveyed the damage. His adrenaline was pumping as he looked up and down the highway, which was a main artery through Ontario. Traffic was backed up for kilometers and there were more than five cars in the mangled wreck as well as a tanker truck, lying on its side across four lanes of the highway.

It was amazing to be in the thick of this. To do his job, but other than nerves he felt nothing and he couldn't help but wonder if he was a bit dead inside.

CHAPTER TWO

"WE NEED TO get this area clear—that tanker is unstable." The fire chief motioned to the tanker.

Samantha nodded. "We almost have all the injured cleared out of the area."

"And we have the traffic both ways being diverted off the highway," the chief of police said.

Samantha looked around at all the carnage. Accidents bothered her. She'd teased George about being sick, but most of the time when they were on their way to large traffic accidents like this she felt a bit queasy too.

Cameron had crashed his ambulance, a mistake that made no sense. So the physicians had investigated why he'd reversed into an empty building and it was then they'd found the tumor. Car accidents made her think back to that awful moment when their lives had changed forever.

While the rest of the team talked about what to do next, Samantha's gaze rested on George through the chaos. She focused on him. He was calm, dealing with victims in an expeditious manner. It was like the rest of the noise, smoke and shouts were drowned out as she watched him. He worked like he was a machine.

They'd worked together at first, but where a new paramedic would have needed guidance, George had known exactly what he was doing.

So she'd let him work on his own. In all her years of mentoring and teaching she knew when to step in and when to step back, and this was one of those moments.

He was down on one knee, patching up a head wound. It was probably an uncomfortable position with one knee on the pavement, but the older lady looked the worse for wear. He was talking to her and she was smiling, even though she was injured.

Even from this distance Samantha could see he was keeping the patient calm. The lady even smiled at him and that made Samantha grin.

Atavik had the touch. He may have been a bit stand-offish and serious with her, but he was good with the patients.

He was meant to be a paramedic.

It was a damn shame he wouldn't move to Critical Care and get back in an aircraft. Though maybe by the end of the course they'd head up to Thunder Bay and perhaps he'd change his tune. She still planned to convince him that it was better in the air.

When you flew planes for as long as Atavik had, it got into your blood. You were born to fly.

George waved at her to signal he was ready for her. She wheeled the gurney over to him and he stood up as she approached.

"I think she's the last one." George turned to the patient. "You ready to get out of here, Mrs. Walker?"

"More than ready, Georgie boy."

Samantha cocked an eyebrow. *Georgie boy?*

George just grinned at Mrs. Walker as he got her to her feet and sitting on the gurney.

"We're going to get you loaded up and off to the hospital."

Samantha and George worked to get Mrs. Walker over to the next departing ambulance as theirs was blocked in by a police cruiser.

Once Mrs. Walker was loaded and the door was shut George slammed on the back to signal to the driver it was okay to leave.

They stepped back as ambulance headed up the newly cleared wrong side of the highway toward the hospital.

The fire crew was waving people away from the tanker, which was beginning to smoke.

"We have to clear out of here. The tanker is unstable," Samantha said.

"I think that's—" The words died in George's throat as a woman let out a gut-wrenching scream. The kind Samantha recognized. The pain of a mother.

"My baby!"

Samantha swung her head to see a little girl, a toddler, running up the highway to the smoking tanker, the firefighters oblivious to her.

The mother was screeching the girl's name but was unable to move because of being strapped to a gurney and getting ready to be transported.

George took one look at the girl and went running.

Samantha reached out to grab him, but her fingertips just brushed George's shirt as he ran through the protesting firefighters and police toward the tanker and the little girl.

"Atavik, get your ass back here!" Samantha shouted, starting after him, but the moment she got close a firefighter grabbed her and held her back.

"Whoa, you can't go."

"I have to. He's my partner. My stupid partner." Samantha pointed in the direction of George.

The firefighter spun round. "He's an idiot."

Samantha's heart was in her throat, her pulse pounding in her ears, as she was forced away and back.

In situations like this, things really did move in slow motion.

She watched as he ran toward the tanker, which burst into flames, knocking the little girl back. He scooped up the terrified girl and started running back to safety as firefighters with hoses ran toward him and then past him to tackle the roaring fire engulfing the remains of the tanker.

He held the little girl against his chest, one protective arm around her head, holding her close as he ran past the fray, like a football player holding a ball tight and streaking towards the end zone.

Samantha's pulse rate eased and she pushed the firefighter away as George made his way toward her. He was panting and there was soot on his face and his arm looked burned.

"You're burned."

"I know." George moved toward, not caring as he delivered the sobbing little girl to her mother.

"Thank you. Oh, God. Thank you." The mother clung to her child, sobbing. "Thank you."

George grinned, nodded and patted the blonde girl's head as she gripped her mother tight.

As two other paramedics wheeled the woman away George groaned and glanced at his arm, cursing under his breath.

Samantha just crossed her arms and glared at him. "Well, looks like we have another patient to take to the hospital. Get in the ambulance, Atavik."

George winced as the ER doctor slathered his burn and then wrapped it.

"You're quite a hero, I hear," she said, as she wrapped his wound. "You're lucky that this wound wasn't more serious."

George winced and then shrugged. "You would've done the same."

His gaze landed on Samantha, who was out in the hall, pacing, angrily. He could tell. He'd seen Charlotte pace just like that.

There was a police officer standing with her, taking notes.

Shoot.

He hoped he wasn't in trouble and on his first day. He didn't want to get booted out of the course. Trainees weren't supposed to do stuff like running toward an exploding tanker. Then another person entered the pantomime and George rolled his eyes.

Good. God.

"George!" Quinn came into the trauma room.

The ER doctor turned and looked. "Family member?"

"Yeah, brother-in-law."

"Only physicians are allowed beyond this point," she said, putting herself between him and Quinn.

"I'm a doctor. Dr. Quinn Devlyn." Quinn pushed past her.

"Devlyn," George said.

"I heard what you did." Quinn shook his head and dragged his hand through his hair. "How am I going to explain that to Charlotte and Mentlana?"

"Don't?" George was confused.

"Too late."

"How the heck did you hear about it? Did my

partner call you? Because, dude, no offense but you're not my emergency contact."

Quinn pinched the bridge of his nose. "You made the national news, you dolt. That's how I found out."

Damn.

"National news?" George rubbed his eyes with his good hand. "I'm in trouble."

"You are that. Charlotte's already called me three times and told me to get to the hospital and kick you in the butt, but also to kiss you. Just so we're clear, I'm not doing that!"

George chuckled. "I appreciate it."

Quinn sighed. "She doesn't want Liv growing up without her uncle."

George chuckled. "Would she prefer it if I dressed in bubble wrap on duty?"

"Your sisters worry about you," Quinn said. "Your partner looks a bit miffed, though."

George glanced over Quinn's shoulder at Samantha, who was openly glaring at him again.

Double damn.

"When are you flying back up to Nunavut?" George asked.

"Tomorrow—why?"

"I may be joining you." George moved his bandaged arm and winced.

"Was it a bad burn?" Quinn looked at Dr. Inkpen.

"No, not too bad." She wrote the discharge information. "Take ibuprofen for the pain and just keep it clean and dry. I trust you know what you're doing, George."

George took the paper she handed to him.

"Thanks, Doctor."

George tucked the discharge sheet into his pocket and climbed out of the chair they'd had him seated on while they'd examined his arm.

"She was cute," Quinn remarked, nudging him in the ribs.

"Dude, are you trying to set me up now?"

Quinn grinned, but then he sobered. "We all worry about you. It's been a year."

George sighed.

He was painfully aware it had been a year.

He knew, because it was burned into his brain as freshly as the day it had happened.

"I don't really want to think about that now."

"Sorry."

"Don't be sorry. How about you buy me a drink before you leave?"

"You don't drink."

George snorted. "I feel like taking it up."

"Well, then, you're in luck. I think there are plenty of people who want to buy you a drink tonight!"

As George stepped into the hall he was met by a round of applause from paramedics, police and firefighters.

It was overwhelming. He hadn't done anything all that spectacular. All he'd done had been to save a life.

Like all of them were taught to do.

George grinned, but it was forced and he hoped no one noticed as he shook countless hands. He didn't like all the attention.

CHAPTER THREE

I SHOULDN'T BE HERE.

That was what Samantha kept telling herself, but somehow she got finagled into going to O'Shea's Pub after George was released from the hospital.

Some of the other paramedics were buying him drinks as was that physician, George's brother-in-law or something, and they were monopolizing his time.

Really, George should be at home getting rest.

You're not his mother.

So she tagged along with the rest of the team to the pub, where George had everyone's attention.

I should go home.

Although Adam was still with her in-laws and wasn't due home for three more hours.

I should go home. Only it was lonely at home

and even after ten years on her own the nights were long and unending.

Sleep didn't come to her easily.

She ordered another whiskey sour and stared up at the television mounted on the wall, watching a replay of what had happened that day.

She hadn't been aware that there had been press there but, then, she'd been focused on getting the injured to the hospital.

"I'll have another iced tea."

Samantha glanced to the side and saw George had come up beside her. "Iced tea?"

George shrugged. "I don't drink and even if I did I shouldn't be anyway, not after my burn."

She was impressed. "Where is your physician brother-in-law?"

"Quinn? He went back to his hotel. He has an early flight back to Iqaluit." George thanked the bartender and tried to slip him a five-dollar bill.

"Nah, man. It's on the house," the barkeeper said.

"Thanks, bro." George took the seat next to

Samantha. "Are you still angry enough to kick me out of the program?"

"No." She chuckled.

George grinned and took a sip of his drink. "Are you telling me you wouldn't have done the same thing?"

He was right. If George hadn't been around and she'd seen that little girl running to the tanker she would've run headlong into the fray and that thought made her feel extremely guilty, because of Adam.

He was already down a father; she couldn't take risks like George or other people.

Adam was her main priority.

And she was kind of jealous of George's freedom.

"I would've." Samantha took another sip of her whiskey sour. "I'm sorry, you deserve the accolades and I'm sorry that I was so hard on you."

George snorted and then frowned. "I don't deserve the accolades. It's part of the job. I'm no hero. Far from it."

Samantha cocked an eyebrow and studied

George. There was a change. He tensed. She could sense he was haunted, conflicted and she couldn't help but wonder about the reason he was so dead set against flying. What was he hiding under that exterior?

Tread carefully, Samantha.

She didn't have time to date or pursue anyone. Not only was she a single mother with a demanding job but she was about to leave town for good. She couldn't let herself get interested in George. He was off limits and, besides, she didn't want to risk her heart. Loving and losing was something she never wanted to experience again.

"How do you like London so far?" she asked, changing the subject.

"It's big."

Samantha smiled. "I guess compared to Iqaluit it would be."

"Things are cheaper."

"What a strange thing to say."

George laughed; she liked the sound of it when he did. "So what's cheaper?"

"Toilet paper," he said. "That stuff is like gold when it's shipped up to Iqaluit, but here you can walk into a store and it won't cost you your firstborn."

Samantha laughed. "Are you really having a conversation with me about toilet paper?"

The twinkle appeared back in his dark eyes. "I guess I am."

Samantha smiled and fiddled with the swizzle stick in her drink. "I've never had a guy approach me in a bar to talk about the price of toilet paper."

"There's a first for everything."

"I guess there is." Her pulse quickened. *Don't flirt. Don't flirt.*

What was it about guys like George that made her hot under the collar? Cameron had been a bit of a rogue too.

Guys like George threw her plan completely out of whack. It drove her crazy, but she also saw the challenge and that was exciting.

"So, should we talk about coupon-clipping

next?" George waggled his eyebrows in a suggestive manner and she laughed uncontrollably.

A belly laugh that made her sides hurt. She couldn't remember the last time she'd laughed like this.

George was dangerous. So very dangerous.

"You have a really nice smile when you genuinely smile," George said, and then he cleared his throat, his smile fading. "Sorry, I didn't mean to say that."

The simple compliment made the butterflies in her stomach flutter and a bit of heat flare in her cheeks. "It's okay and thanks."

She was attracted to him.

This is going to end badly.

The last thing she needed to be doing was checking out a man. Especially when that particular man was off limits.

She was his mentor.

I don't have time to date, she reminded herself again. She was leaving for Thunder Bay. Any relationship would be temporary and with a son she couldn't have a temporary romance. She wouldn't subject Adam to that.

And it wasn't just Adam. She didn't want a temporary romance. It was too risky for her heart.

She really needed to get out of there.

"Is something wrong?" George asked.

"No, why would you ask that?"

"The expression on your face."

"Yeah, it was one heck of a day."

George stopped smiling as he took a sip of his iced tea.

I've got to get out of here.

"Well, I'd better head home." She downed the rest of her whiskey sour and stood up.

"How are you getting home?"

"Bus," Samantha said. "I live in the south end."

"Let me walk you out."

"You don't have to—"

"I want to," he said, and he said it in a way that brooked no argument.

As they headed to the door someone called out, "You leaving already, Atavik?"

George turned. "No, just walking Doxtator out and then I'll be back!"

Samantha groaned inwardly. Now they were the center of attention. She should just tell George to stay, but she doubted he would listen to her. Since he'd been assigned to her, he hadn't listened to her.

He was determined and his hand rested gently against the small of her back as he walked her up the stairs to street level.

It was May and the sun was starting to sink in the west and the lights were glowing as twilight crept across the city.

There was a warm breeze, but it wasn't hot; it was refreshing.

"It's hot out here," said George. "I don't think I'll get used to the heat."

Samantha grinned. "Just like I don't think many of us would get used to your cold."

George smiled, but, as ever, it faded quickly.

"Are you sure you don't want to stick around for a bit longer?"

"No, thank you. I need to get home."

"Why?"

"Adam will be home soon."

Then she saw the expression that passed across most men's face when she mentioned Adam's name. He was trying to process it and there was a flare of jealousy mixed with disappointment before he caught the range of emotions and hid them.

Who was Adam? was his first thought and his second was, Why should he care?

It wasn't any of his business. A woman as beautiful as Samantha would, of course, have a husband or boyfriend. Besides, she was off limits—a fact he needed to keep reminding himself of.

He wasn't interested. He wasn't going to get involved with anyone again, it was too risky. Still, the green-eyed monster couldn't help but rear its ugly little head. Samantha was beautiful, intriguing and he wished she wasn't his mentor. He wished she was single, in a bar and he was just meeting her. Trying to pick her up.

But who was he kidding? Cheryl had killed that side of him. He had vowed never to love again, to never put his heart at risk. He'd promised himself that in the hospital. He was trying to keep from flirting with Samantha, but he couldn't help himself.

"It's okay to date again, George. You need to move on. You have a right to."

Only he shook his sister Mentlana's words out of his head. No. He didn't deserve love again. He didn't want it again.

Get a grip on yourself.

Why was he letting himself think like this? It was dumb. Sure, he was attracted to Samantha but that didn't mean anything had to happen.

Except she was the first woman he'd been really attracted to since Cheryl.

They walked down the street to the empty bus stop.

"You have a training session tomorrow morning at seven sharp, and I'll see you in the afternoon," Samantha said. "Try to get that through to the other paramedics too."

George laughed. "I will."

Samantha stopped and jammed her hands in her pockets. "You can head back to O'Shea's."

George shook his head. "No, I think I'll just wait here with you." He was treading on dangerous ground but he couldn't resist it.

Pink bloomed in her cheeks.

He cleared his throat and looked at her. She was so beautiful. He needed to get away. Fast.

Only he couldn't move. He stayed there, standing close to her. Close enough to touch.

Run.

Only he didn't run. Instead, he imagined what it would be like to kiss her. Her lips looked soft, moist and he wondered if they tasted as sweet as he imagined.

"I should go. You're right. I'm sure your boyfriend Adam will be glad to see you're home safe."

Samantha still didn't say anything—she didn't

have a chance as the bus pulled up and opened its doors. She climbed up the first step.

You're an idiot, Atavik.

George waited for a word from her.

Anything.

Even "Scram" would suffice.

Instead, she smiled, the pink in her cheeks still shining. "I'm not involved with anyone. Adam is my son."

And with that the doors of the bus closed with a hiss and George watched as it took off down the street.

He grinned, relieved to hear Adam was her son, but it didn't last long. If there was a child there was a father.

She's off limits.

He would keep his distance. That wasn't what he wanted to do but it would be the best thing. He was here to learn, not date, and not fall in love with someone. He'd tried love once and it had nearly broken him.

He wouldn't make that mistake twice.

CHAPTER FOUR

SAMANTHA HAD THOUGHT George was going to kiss her, but he hadn't and she was both relieved and disappointed.

It had been a long time since she'd had a kiss. Though she didn't know why she was allowing disappointment to gnaw at her. She'd only just met George and she was his mentor. Still, she couldn't deny the spark he'd ignited inside her. A slow-burning ember making her feel giddy. It was a scary prospect indeed.

It had been the moment he'd come running down the highway, cradling that child, putting himself in danger to save that little girl.

That was it. It wasn't attraction, it was a motherly instinct that played with her.

Nice try, Samantha.

When she'd married Cameron, she'd sworn to herself that he would be her first and her last.

She just hadn't expected their last kiss to come so soon.

She had been expecting fifty years or more.

Not the just the five they'd had.

It hadn't been enough.

Then George had shown up, turning her world upside down, and she wished he'd kissed her. But that would not have been wise.

A year after Cameron had died his mother, Joyce, had told her that it was okay for her to move on. That she was too young to spend the rest of her life alone.

Samantha had been horrified by that prospect.

She hadn't been able to even contemplate finding someone else or loving again.

Cameron had been gone ten years now. She thought about moving on, even though it was scary to let someone else in.

Samantha touched her lips, which still tingled in anticipation. The heady scent of his skin wrapped around her. He'd been so close and just thinking about what might've happened flustered her.

Get a grip on yourself. He has no interest in you. You're delusional.

It was effect of the drinks she had still in her system. It was making her out of sorts. Yes, that was it. She was going to blame it on the alcohol, even though she hadn't imbibed that much of it, but it was a good scapegoat.

She headed into the bathroom and turned on the cold water, splashing it against her face. Maybe she could wash it all away.

She cleaned her face and then undid her hair from the high ponytail, brushing it out so it wouldn't get snarled.

Still, she couldn't get George out of her mind, which was going to make it hard to be his mentor.

When Cameron's parents brought Adam home they spoke to her and she made pleasantries, but she was sure she sounded like she was a zombie.

Yes. No. Uh-huh. And that was thanks to George.

They asked if she was okay several times and she finally told them she was just tired, that a large car crash on the highway had left her exhausted. They understood and left.

Adam, however, didn't understand his mother's distraction.

And she couldn't blame him.

This was not how she usually acted. Being like this drove her crazy.

"What's with you tonight, Mom?" Adam asked, giving her a wary look.

"Nothing. Nothing's wrong with me. Why would you ask?"

Adam shrugged. "You looked weird and zoned out."

"I'm fine."

Adam nodded, no longer interested. Why would he suspect that being in close proximity to a handsome man she had just met had apparently melted her brain into the consistency of fondue. Gooey, stringy fondue.

These feelings were old, but foreign and unwelcome.

It was bad timing.

"Hey, Mom, can I go over to Ameer's house?"

"No," she said to Adam. "You have to go to school tomorrow. Let's get you to bed."

"Do I have to?"

"Yes."

The subject of bed distracted Adam, so much so that he didn't question her trance-like state and she even forgot for a few moments as she wrestled her son into bed.

It was when the lights were out and she was lying in bed that the fantasy of a kiss come flooding back to her. Night-time was always hard on her anyway. The bed felt so empty even after all this time.

Tonight it felt like she was even more alone. She tossed and turned all night long, making it a large cup of coffee type of morning when she got up at five and got Adam up and out to the school's daycare.

When she got to work, she wasn't even sure how she'd got across the city. She couldn't remember anything about her drive there, and that was bad. She didn't like losing control over herself. This was getting ridiculous.

Get a grip on yourself.

"Afternoon, Sam. How was the first day?"

What? She stared down at the paper coffee cup in her hand, thinking it had spoken to her and she was cracking up.

"Yo! Earth to Sam!"

Samantha turned and Lizzie was giving her a strange look.

"What?"

Lizzie raised one of her eyebrows and crossed her arms. "I asked how the first day went."

"Why do you ask it like that?"

"Like what?"

"Evilly."

Lizzie smirked. "I *know* how it went. The hospital's report on a certain paramedic's burn came in to process through the company's insurance."

Samantha groaned. "George's?"

Then Lizzie reached over and held up the newspaper.

Samantha had to do a double-take at the large picture on the front of the newspaper. It was

George, running through the line of firemen that was headed to the wall of flames behind him, and in his arms was that sweet little girl cradled against his chest.

The headline was "Hero Paramedic".

Samantha took the paper from Lizzie's hand and scanned the article quickly.

"I guess he had a successful first day." Lizzie leaned against her desk. "Not every day a newbie to the program can hit such heights of heroics."

"Yeah, he did a good job." Samantha handed the paper back to Lizzie. "Hopefully he won't get a swollen head and prance around here like he owns the place."

"I don't think Atavik is that type of person, do you?"

No. He wasn't and Samantha knew that.

Still, coverage like this would go to anyone's head. Even though he denied the fact, he was a hero.

Like the word "hero" was a burden to him.

Lizzie chuckled. "What have you got on your mind?"

"Nothing," Samantha responded, but Lizzie didn't look convinced. "Has he arrived?"

Lizzie nodded. "Yeah, he's in the other room."

Samantha headed into the common room. She caught sight of George sitting across the room, his head bent over a manual, studying.

"Good afternoon!" She grinned and tried not to look at George, because she knew if she looked his way then she'd start blushing again.

And she didn't want to. It was bad enough he rendered her into a space cadet.

She didn't want him know how much he affected her.

The room was painfully silent, but she could sense that George was looking at her and her cheeks heated.

Dammit. Come on. Focus.

She was better than this. She was level-headed and in control.

"Did you get home okay?" she asked after she cleared her throat to keep her voice steady, because she was sure if she didn't it would crack like that of some pubescent boy.

George nodded. "I did. Thanks." The cheeky grin from the night before was gone. He was professional and though it was a relief that it was all business, like nothing had passed between them, it still stung her.

There was an awkward silence.

Say something. Say anything.

"Well, we have a patient transfer this afternoon." She cleared her throat. "It should be pretty straightforward."

"Where are we headed?" he asked.

"We have to up to Goderich to get her." Samantha poured herself another cup of coffee.

"How far is that?"

Samantha cocked an eyebrow. "Do you have other plans?"

George shook his head. "No, just curious."

Samantha wasn't convinced that it was just curiosity. He looked agitated at the prospect of being alone with her.

"Goderich is almost two hours there, give or

take, and then it depends on traffic and the hospital, but expect this trip to take most of the day."

George nodded and slung his knapsack over his shoulder, and as he did that Samantha saw his bandaged arm.

"How's your arm this morning?"

"It's a bit sore."

Samantha set down her coffee cup and walked over to him, taking his arm gently. "Can I look?"

"Sure."

Sure?

Why had he agreed to let her touch him?

He should've said no, because he hadn't slept a wink last night and it hadn't been the pain meds or the burn that had kept him up.

It had been Samantha.

He could smell her perfume as he stood close to her.

Heather, the sweet smell of summer on the tundra.

The part he'd thought had died with Cheryl

long ago had come alive, and lambasted him for not taking Samantha in his arms and kissing her. When she'd mentioned Adam yesterday the green-eyed monster had reared his head.

And then she'd told him Adam was her son.

He'd had no idea she was a mother.

Not that that was a deal-breaker. Far from it. He was just surprised.

If there had of been a third paramedic going with them to Goderich, it would have been a welcome distraction. But there wasn't and he'd be trapped in an ambulance with Samantha for several hours. Which was the last thing he wanted. It was going to be absolute torture not to reach out and touch her, kiss her, and he hated himself for being weak.

You're here to do a job.

He wasn't here to romance. He wasn't looking for a significant other. He was here to learn as much as he could so when he took a posting with the company in Thunder Bay he could do his job well.

Though it wouldn't be as far up north as he

liked. For that he'd have to climb into a plane again and he wasn't going to do that. It had been bad enough flying down here, but then he hadn't been the pilot.

He had been able to take something to help him relax, letting Quinn get him on and off the plane.

George closed his eyes as the sounds of the crash filled his head.

The howling wind, listening for the sound of a polar bear as he'd dragged his limp body across the snow to dig himself a shelter, certain he was going to die.

Not now.

He took a deep breath and silenced the voices.

"Am I hurting you?"

Then he realized that Samantha was touching him.

He'd forgotten momentarily that she was looking at his burn. Her long, delicate fingers were touching his tender skin with a feather-light touch that ignited his blood.

"No, you're not hurting me. I mean, it's tender, but you're not hurting me."

"Well, it looks fine and you're keeping the salve on. That's good." She smiled up at him.

"My adopted sister is a doctor, she'd kick my butt if I didn't follow doctor's orders."

Samantha chuckled and then wrapped his burn back up and let go of him, taking a step back. "I forgot there's a lot of medical people in your family. Is the adopted sister the one Dr. Devlyn is married to?"

"Yes." George pulled down his shirtsleeve and buttoned the cuff. "Charlotte was the daughter of our village's physician, but he died when Charlotte was young and she had no other family so my family took her in. She became a physician like her father and came up to Cape Recluse to practice and I was her paramedic."

"Very tight-knit community."

"Very." *You don't know the half of it.*

Samantha tucked an errant strand of ebony hair behind her ear. "Well, we'd better get a move on. The run to Goderich will take most of the day."

Damn.

"Of course. Lead the way."

Samantha, still not looking at him, turned on her heel and George followed her out to the garage where the ambulances were kept.

Today was going to be a long day.

A long and trying day as he battled the part of him that told him to reach out and kiss her. The traitorous side he'd thought he'd buried with Cheryl's memories.

CHAPTER FIVE

IT WAS ABSOLUTE TORTURE, being in the ambulance with him. No words were exchanged because she wasn't going to encourage conversation. It was better this way. Professional.

It was horrible.

He was so close. The warmth of his body firing her blood, making her pulse race. She felt like a girl who'd never been kissed. Any movement from him made her heart skip a beat, her body reacting to him. She wondered if he'd take her in his arms and do what she'd been fantasizing he'd do.

Oh, dear.

Maybe focusing on her career for so long hadn't been the right course. Maybe if she'd dated more, gotten out more, she wouldn't be acting this way. Only she hadn't had any desire to date. No one had piqued her fancy.

Until George.

"What lake is that?" George asked, looking in her direction.

"Lake Huron."

"Wow, the water is so blue!"

Samantha grinned. Goderich sat on a bluff and at certain points you could see Lake Huron. Even after a tornado had devastated the town, it was still one of the prettiest spots for miles. At least, that was her opinion.

"What color were you expecting it to be?" Samantha asked.

"I don't know." George grinned and glanced at her. "I guess grey."

"Grey?"

"The first great lake I came across was Lake Ontario. I was visiting my sister in Toronto when she was going to medical college. I guess I just assumed they'd all be the same."

"Tsk-tsk. You judged a book by its cover."

George rolled his eyes and shook his head and she just laughed. He was so easygoing, but it was only rare times she saw this side of him. Usually he was aloof and distant and she couldn't help but wonder which side of him was real.

Was it the stand-offish, polite version or that charming funny man with the dark twinkling eyes who made her heart skip a beat?

What was hiding beneath that veneer.

There was just something she couldn't quite put her finger on, but she felt like maybe the aloof act was a wall meant to keep people out.

Nothing more was said as they drove into town and straight over to the hospital, where they parked at the emergency entrance.

"Do you have the paperwork?" she asked George as she put the ambulance in park and undid her seat belt.

"Right here." George waved the clipboard and climbed out of the ambulance.

Samantha followed, but before they entered the hospital they were met by a physician.

"You the crew coming to transport Doris Hall-man?"

"Yes," Samantha said. "We're to take her down to the hospital in London."

"I'm sorry, we called but you had already left and your crew couldn't get hold of you. Mrs. Hallman passed away early this morning. There's no need for a patient transfer."

"I'm sorry to hear that." Then Samantha couldn't help but wonder what the heck had happened to her radio since Dispatch hadn't been able to get through.

"If you could sign off on this paperwork," George said, handing the doctor the clipboard. Once the paperwork was squared away they got back in the ambulance and headed back to London.

As they headed out of town George picked up the radio and tried to call back to the base, but there was no response. There wasn't even static.

"That's weird." Samantha frowned. "That's never happened before."

"What do you think happened here?" George asked, hanging the receiver back on the dashboard.

"I don't—"

She had been about to tell him she didn't

know, but the engine light came on and smoke started to rise from the engine.

She cursed quietly under her breath, as she pulled off to the side of the road and put on her four-way lights. As soon as she put the ambulance in park the engine seized and made a horrific grinding sound, before it died away completely in a puff of smoke.

Just. Great.

"Well, I guess we have our answer," George said.

George leapt out of the ambulance and Samantha popped the hood before following him out.

"What do you think caused it?" Samantha asked, as she waved away the lingering smoke.

"My first guess is an oil leak." George cocked his head sideways. "That might be why the electrical unit failed and the radio malfunctioned."

"Are you any good with repairs?"

George scratched his head. "With planes, but I don't know much about ambulance maintenance. Even if I did, there's not much we can do if the engine died on us."

She groaned. Great. She was going to be late picking up Adam from the sitter. And when she'd promised him that she wouldn't be late tonight. The run up to Goderich was supposed to be simple.

She pulled out her cellphone and it was dead too.

Dammit.

She'd forgot to charge the stupid thing.

"My phone is dead. I forgot to charge it." Samantha pocketed it again. "Can I borrow your cell?"

"I don't have a phone," George said.

Samantha cocked an eyebrow. "You don't have a phone?"

"You say that with such disbelief." George chuckled. "I have a land line at my apartment but not a cellphone."

"I can't believe you don't have a phone."

"Why is that so hard to grasp?" he asked.

"Doesn't everyone?"

"Apparently not."

She could tell he wasn't pleased with this situation either. He ran his hand over his head and let out a whispered curse word. She couldn't blame him. She felt like cursing too, but they were stuck and she figured one of them would soon have to start walking.

A pickup truck with agricultural plates slowed down and a weathered old farmer rolled down the window. "Need some help?"

"Can we borrow your phone?" Samantha asked.

George leaned in. "The guy rolled down his window. You honestly think he has a cell…" The words died in his throat and Samantha had to stifle a smug smile as the farmer held out his smartphone.

She quickly keyed in the number for Dispatch.

"Health Land and Air. Please state the nature of your call." It was Lizzie on the other end, thank goodness.

"It's Doxtator, Ambulance 29956."

"Samantha, what happened? We've been trying to get hold of you for a while."

"The radio was offline. I think there was an

electrical malfunction, but the ambulance's engine has seized and we're stranded at the side of the road."

"The hospital called just after you left. We tried to call you back, but we couldn't get hold of you."

"Sorry." And she was.

If the damn radio had worked, if her cell had been charged, she wouldn't be trapped with George on the side of the road.

"It's okay. We're glad you're okay. Where are you located?" Lizzie asked.

"About five kilometers south of Goderich on Highway 21."

"Okay, we're dispatching a tow truck to your location and we'll send another transport up to get you and George."

Samantha ended the call and handed the phone back to the farmer. "Thanks for your help."

"Not a problem. Do you need a lift somewhere?" the farmer asked.

"No, a tow truck will be coming." She motioned over her shoulder. "We have to stay with the ambulance."

The farmer tipped his hat. "Glad to have been of some help." He drove away and she wandered over to the side of the road.

George was leaning against a picket fence, a piece of grass in his mouth which he was chewing. She chuckled.

"What's up?" he asked.

"You look like a hick."

"Well, apparently, according to you I am one because I don't have a cellphone." A brief smile played on his lips and she resisted the urge to tell him she preferred him this way. She didn't particularly like the serious side of him.

Samantha like the boyish charm that snuck out every once in a while. The side he was apparently fighting hard to keep in.

She'd had enough seriousness in her life.

Cameron had been a joker. Their life had been full of love and laughter, until the tumor had come and the Cameron she'd loved had disappeared.

"This treatment will help. You'll see." She *tried to reach out and take his hand, but Cameron snatched it away.*

"Don't touch me. Just leave me alone." His *eyes no longer sparkled. They were dark, hollow. His body frail and all the humor gone, leached away by the tumor.*

"So why do I look like a hick?" George asked, breaking into her thoughts.

"The grass in your mouth."

George tossed it away. "What did Dispatch say?"

"Dispatch is sending a tow truck and another ambulance is coming to pick us up."

"How long will that take?" he asked brusquely. He sounded put out, the jovial side of him gone again.

"I don't know. Are you in a rush?"

"Not particularly."

Silence fell between them and an uneasy tension, which made Samantha uncomfortable in a way she wished she could explore further.

Don't think about it.

George chuckled to himself, breaking the tension between them.

"What's so funny?" she asked.

"I really didn't think that guy would have a phone, let alone a smartphone."

"He showed you up, didn't he?" Samantha winked. "I think you're the odd man out, not having a cellphone."

He shrugged. "I really don't want one."

Samantha sighed and then remembered her sitter. "Oh, shoot, I should've called my sitter to let her know I was going to be late."

"Well, whoever picks us up should have a phone you can borrow. Hopefully they'll be here soon." George glanced up at the sky. "At least it's a nice day."

"True. It could be raining."

"Don't say that, or it will happen. We seem to be cursed today." There was a twinkle in his eyes. The twinkle made her weak in the knees. The look that made her feel carefree and young again, not that she was particularly over the hill at thirty-three.

"Thanks for that." She sighed again. "Too bad we didn't break down in town."

George shrugged. "Why? It's nice around here. There's fields and a view of the blue water."

Samantha laughed. "You and the blue water."

"It's not like I'm not used to blue water. I'm just used to it being salt water and not fresh." He turned and looked behind him, holding out his arms wide. "I mean, it's pretty impressive."

I think where you come from is pretty amazing. But instead of saying the thought out loud she asked, "So what made you decide to come down here?"

"I want to learn to drive a land ambulance and become a paramedic in a city or town. Hopefully I'll get to stay in Thunder Bay."

"You want to stay up north?"

George nodded. "Yeah, I don't think I could give it up. The north is in my blood."

"Then why don't you become a—?"

"I don't want to fly." The easygoing demeanor disappeared. The twinkle in his eyes was gone.

His whole body tensed, like a taut rope being pulled and ready to snap.

"I'm sorry, I didn't mean to bring it up again. It's just a lot of Ontario's north is only accessible by plane."

"I know," he said quietly. "I know, but my decision is made." George began to walk along the side of the road. His back was ramrod straight, his body tense as he kicked at the gravel shoulder.

She regretted bringing up the subject again, but it ate at her curiosity. He wanted to work in the north, he was passionate about his job and he had a pilot's license. Only he didn't want to fly any longer.

Had something happened up there in the air?

Something must have affected him profoundly.

Who am I to pry?

Who indeed?

Cameron's death had affected her. It had taken so long to get back into a routine. For years she'd felt like she was living her life on autopilot. Which was no way to live. She wasn't ever sure she was even off autopilot yet. She'd become so used to the way her life was.

It was another reason why she wanted to fly, to work in the near north. She wanted to get out of the city and away from cars, roads. She just wanted to escape it all. Maybe then she'd find herself again.

But some would say she was running away from her problems, just as much as George might be running away from his.

He obviously didn't want to talk about it and she had no right to pry. She was his mentor, but that was it. She was nothing more to him.

Samantha crossed her arms and ambled over to him. He'd opened the back of the ambulance and was sitting in the back, his feet on the bumper, his head hanging.

"I'm sorry for trying to pry. Again."

George looked up. His expression was resolved and relaxed, but that sparkle of devil-may-care was gone.

"It's okay."

Samantha took a seat next to him. "What's living up in Iqaluit like?"

"Cold."

Samantha smiled and glanced at him. The twinkle was back. "I gathered."

George shrugged. "It's home. I miss it, but I like it here too. At least here when you get into a cab they don't try to sell you turkeys."

What?

"What?" she asked.

George laughed at her expression, which she was positive was comical, because for the life of her she couldn't connect the need for a taxi with a turkey.

"Did you say turkey?"

George nodded. "Food is so expensive up there that cab drivers have been known, near the holidays, to get a job lot of turkeys from wholesalers who ship them up at a deep discount. Then they try to sell the turkeys cheaper than the store does, but of course at a profit. I met three different cabbies two Christmases ago who were all trying to sell me a turkey."

"Taxi turkey?"

"You got it. It was good turkey too."

Samantha laughed. "You bought a taxi turkey?"

George shrugged. "Sure, why not? It was still frozen in the trunk. Where else was I going to get it?"

"I guess I take it for granted that our taxi drivers don't have to sell turkeys on the side."

"Exactly my point." George grinned and looked off into the distance. "It really was good turkey, though."

"Was it air-freshener flavored?"

He laughed at that. A large booming laugh that made her join in. They laughed until her sides hurt. It had been a long time since she'd just let go and laughed like that.

The last time she'd relaxed like that had been with Cameron.

They'd been at the beach in Grand Bend. It hadn't even been summer, it had been fall and the seemingly endless stretches of white sandy beaches, which usually teemed with tourists and beachgoers in the summer, had been nearly empty.

They had been relaxing on the sand, watching the breakers crash against the shore, and she'd turned and whispered to him, telling him he was going to be a father for the first time.

Ten months later, they'd found out Cameron had had the brain tumor. Six months after he had gone.

She stood and crossed her arms, trying to focus on the road north, willing the tow truck to come, but instead all she saw were waves of heat shimmering off the tarmac.

"You okay?" George asked.

"Of course. Why wouldn't I be?" She didn't look back at him, but she could feel his gaze on her, boring into her back.

"You seem tense."

"Just thinking about my late husband. He loved Lake Huron."

George's eyes widened. "You're a widow?"

Samantha nodded. "For ten years."

Then she cleared her throat, uncomfortable

with the course of this conversation. She didn't usually open up to people about Cameron. People who got involved in your personal life became friends and then you become emotionally invested and vulnerable to pain and hurt.

Yet she'd opened up to George, she'd shared that piece of Cameron with him, and she didn't know why.

"I can't believe I didn't notice the ambulance was in disrepair," she said, quickly changing the subject.

"Look, you couldn't have known there was going to be an electrical failure and the engine giving out. Just be thankful that the patient wasn't on board."

The tension in Samantha's shoulders melted away. "I'm sorry, this has never happened to me before."

George cocked an eyebrow. "You've never had a car go south on you before? I find that hard to believe."

She grinned. "You find it hard to believe? You've already proved your sense of judgment isn't that sound since you thought an old farmer wouldn't have a cellphone."

He acted like he was outraged with a small huff and a slight shake of his head, but she knew he was bluffing.

She admired his laid-back attitude, his ability to take things as they came. She wandered back to the ambulance and sat down beside him again.

"I really wish the tow truck would come so I could call Adam." She pinched the bridge of her nose. "I know he'll understand. He's a good kid, but I hate always leaving him in the lurch. Always running late, missing stuff. It's just so hard, being a single parent."

"No doubt."

Samantha glanced up at George. "I feel like a terrible mother sometimes."

This time when George shook his head it wasn't an act. "I doubt that very much. You said he understands. How old is he?"

"Ten."

George's eyes widened. "You are not old enough to have a ten-year-old kid."

Samantha snorted. "That's a terrible line."

"Was I using a line on you?"

Samantha's cheeks flushed and when she glanced up at him she realized how close he was to her. So close that all she had to do was lean in just a wee bit and their lips would be touching.

What am I doing? Kiss him, you idiot.

Maybe if she did, she wouldn't be so anxious around him.

Kiss him and be done with it.

Instead of taking the chance, though, she cleared her throat and backed away, staring at her knees and the shadow the ambulance cast in the long grass on the side of the highway.

What was it about George? What was it about him that made her let go of her inhibitions? She glanced at him, leaning against the door, staring up at the sky.

There was something mysterious about it. Something that called to her, like George understood her pain. Only he didn't. George wasn't a widower.

Still, he made her forget, he made her feel carefree, and that thought scared her.

"Man, I do like the sun, but it's freaking hot."

"Hot? It's only twenty degrees out."

"You forget again where I come from. Twenty is *hot*." And he put the emphasis on "hot".

"Well, you just have to cut across the field there and you can jump in the lake, though it's still pretty cold."

"I would so do it."

"I don't doubt that." Samantha leaned back against the other open door and stared up at the blue sky dotted with fat, fluffy, white clouds.

"I'm glad we have the weekend off," George said, breaking the silence that had fallen between them.

"Me too."

Silence descended again, making her feel uncomfortable.

"Is everyone in your family medically inclined?" she asked, hoping to ease the tension.

George nodded. "Pretty much. Well, not Mentlana. She was a teacher and then she had a baby. I'm sure she'll go back to it, but she's had some health issues for a while."

"Does her husband work?"

"He works the ice roads and then in the summer he works on a fishing boat. My grandmother was an artist."

"Oh, really? Would I know her?"

George grinned. "Are you familiar with Inuit art?"

She blushed. "Sorry, not really."

"It's okay, not many are, but there's some of her stuff in the local museum."

"You'll have to show me." The words slipped out of her mouth before she thought about them.

Great way to keep your distance, Samantha.

"Yeah, maybe." George cleared his throat and moved away. It was subtle, but she noticed it.

He wasn't interested in her. Why would she think he was?

"Sorry, you don't have to."

His brow furrowed in confusion. "No, it's

okay. I don't mind showing you my grandmother's stuff. She was a pretty awesome lady."

"Oh, I'm sorry. When did she pass?" She was relieved to change the subject. Even for a moment.

"Two winters ago, but she lived a good life. She was over a hundred."

Samantha's eyes widened. "That's amazing."

"Yeah, it is." George's gaze turned north. "I see flashing lights. I think it's our tow truck."

Samantha looked where he was pointing and saw the lights flashing up the highway. She was relieved that help was coming fairly quickly, but on the other hand she was kind of sad that their little time alone on the side of the highway was over.

She'd enjoyed their time together. It was a nice day and she hadn't had a moment to just sit down and watch the world go by in a long time.

Still, this was better, because once they went up north next month she'd go off to the flight portion, he'd be on the road and then they would be assigned to different locations.

That's a feeble excuse.

It had nothing to do with physical location. It was emotional. Though she'd long ago mourned Cameron, it was not his memory that held her back but the recollection of the pain. The tattered state of her heart when he had died.

Her heart had taken a long time to heal. To mend, so that the pain wasn't sharp but dull. A pain that eventually dissipated and she could manage.

She wasn't willing to risk putting her heart through anything like that again.

There was no future for them.

There couldn't be.

And it was for the best.

CHAPTER SIX

SHE'S SLEEPING ON ME.

George glanced over at Samantha, her head resting on his shoulder as they sat in the back of the ambulance that had come to take them back to London. At least Samantha had now been able to call home. She had been so worried about her son and George didn't blame her in the least.

Her concern for her son warmed his heart. He could only imagine the strain of having to be both mother and father to Adam and hold down a pressurized job.

He understood about stress. Especially during times when you didn't think it was affecting you at all, but it was doing a number on your body. Making you feel sick, tired until you just crashed.

He'd been there.

Too many times.

He didn't blame her for falling asleep in the back. The rhythmic rocking of the ambulance was enough to make him stifle a yawn or two.

Though he should wake her up and move her off his shoulder, he liked her being so close. It was taking all his willpower not to reach out and wrap his arm around her. Although it would be more ideal if they were on a comfy couch or even in a bed.

The thought of cuddling her in bed made his blood heat.

Don't think of her like that. She's off limits.

He was horrible for thinking that way.

George glanced down at the top of her head again. The comforting scent of her shampoo didn't help matters. It made him think of home. Of summers and endless daylight, blue skies and the ice breaking in the bay.

Think about taxi turkey.

Even thinking about something as strange and random as a cab driver selling him a frozen turkey out of the trunk of his car did little to deter his thoughts from the inevitable, and that inevitable was Samantha.

Why did he always go for the unobtainable women?

It was a weakness of his, but he couldn't help himself.

A woman he could never have. *Only because you won't have her.*

And even that wasn't entirely true, because he wanted her and with such a fiery need it scared him. The last time he'd wanted a woman like this it had ended up leaving him broken. He'd sworn it hadn't been worth it. What was it about Samantha that made him think differently?

He saw something in her, something she didn't see in herself, and that was strength.

Samantha worried about being a good mother and even though he didn't know her son, he knew that she was devoted enough that she wasn't a bad mother.

His mother had been a workaholic, but she had always made time for them. She'd always doted on them, even if she'd had to leave because of an emergency, and he hadn't been any worse off for being her son.

Of course, he'd had a father too.

Samantha was all alone.

He couldn't figure out why she was so determined to work as an air paramedic. He closed his eyes and tried to drown out the sound of his plane's engine failing, the sight of snow filling his windshield as the plane plummeted to the ground.

George swallowed the lump in his throat and banished those thoughts far from his mind. He wouldn't let them bother him again.

He did miss flying, though.

Truly, he did.

He missed the far north. He missed making an impact and helping out his community.

He missed his family.

London was a big place. Not huge, but big enough to make him feel just a touch uncomfortable.

When he flew it was just him, the plane and the sky. Lots of wide open spaces. He often dreamt of flying again, but the dream always ended with the crash and Cheryl.

Then he was angry at himself for thinking about Cheryl. For letting her in where she didn't belong.

Don't let the memories in.

There was a jolt, a bump in the highway, and Samantha moaned slightly, her head flopping the other way.

He laughed silently to himself. Her cheek had the crease of his white uniform shirt in her skin and she was still perfect. But he couldn't have her.

Their lives were going on separate paths. He knew where he had to go and she was going to pursue her dream to be a pilot.

When she headed to the airport outside Thunder Bay, he would be stationed right downtown in the city's core.

Then, after six months, who knew where he would end up. He'd like to stay in Thunder Bay, but he might be transferred. *Pathetic excuse.* He was lying to himself. It was better to keep his distance from her. Better for his heart.

He had to be unselfish and detach himself emotionally from her.

All they could be was work colleagues.

Yes, that's all they could be. Yet every time he gave himself this pep talk he found himself drawn in and engaged.

Her eyelids fluttered open. "Where are we?" She was groggy still.

"Almost there," George whispered.

Samantha nodded and then rubbed her eyes. "I've got to wake up. I have to drive home after this."

"No, you're not going to drive anywhere. You're exhausted. I'll take you home."

He cursed inward to himself. *What are you doing? This is not distancing yourself.*

"What? No, I can't ask you to do that."

"Yeah, you can."

Samantha smiled and leaned her head back against the headrest. "Okay."

He was a doomed man.

* * *

"You drove me home when I was barely conscious. The least you can do is come in and use the phone."

George shook his head. "It's okay, the mall is just over there."

He was right. Her place was right across from the mall, but why go there when she had a perfectly good phone here?

"No, come in."

He seemed hesitant and then he said, "Okay, just to use your phone."

Samantha raised an eyebrow at the strange statement. What else did he expect would happen? She unlocked the security door and they entered the lobby of her apartment. George headed for the elevator.

"I'm actually just down the hall here. I have a main-floor apartment."

"Convenient."

Samantha smiled. "Yeah, it's pretty nice."

It wasn't the house she'd always dreamed she'd have at this stage in her life. She didn't have a fenced backyard or an elaborate garden, that house was in Thunder Bay. Still, the patio was good, and in the summer it was nice to have a few plants and do some barbecuing.

She unlocked the door and paused as the light was on. She hadn't left the light on when she'd left.

"Hey, Mom!" Adam came running from his bedroom.

"Adam, what're you doing home? I thought you were at Sherry's?"

"Grandma picked me up. Sherry called her and let her know you got stuck in Goderich, so Grandma picked me up and here I am." Adam peered around her. "Who's that?"

Darn.

She'd momentarily forgotten that George was standing right behind her. What next?

"Samantha, I'm glad you're home." Cameron's mother, Joyce, walked in from the living room and stopped as well when she saw George. "Oh, I'm sorry, I didn't know you had company."

Samantha groaned inwardly.

"I'm George, Samantha's partner. She's mentoring me during my training and she's letting me borrow the phone."

Cameron's mother smiled. "Pleased to meet you, George."

George nodded and then looked at Adam. "You must be Adam."

"Yeah," Adam responded.

"Your mother speaks highly of you." Then he turned to her. "Where's your phone?"

"Just in the living room." Samantha pointed in the direction of the phone.

George nodded. "Excuse me." He moved past her mother-in-law and her son and headed in the living room.

"I'm sorry, I didn't know you'd be here," Samantha murmured as she brushed back Adam's hair from his forehead.

Joyce shook her head. "Why are you apologizing? Anyway, I'll say goodnight." She bent over and gave Adam a quick kiss, much to his chagrin.

"Thanks again, Joyce, for picking him up."

Joyce grinned and then hugged Samantha. "Any time."

When she left Samantha locked the door and let out a sigh of relief. Until she heard voices coming from the living room and realized Adam and George were talking.

This was not keeping her relationship with George professional.

Cool your jets. Lots of coworkers have met Adam, she told herself. It was true, but she'd never been attracted to any of her coworkers before.

The couple of times she'd gone on a date with a man, at the insistence of Joyce, she'd never let him meet Adam because she hadn't wanted Adam to get attached to someone who wouldn't be around forever.

Adam had already lost enough.

"Cameron wouldn't have wanted you to remain alone forever. You're too young, Samantha, and Adam needs a father."

Those had been Joyce's words a year after Cameron's death. It was true. She could move on.

Still, she couldn't bring herself to even contemplate such a notion. Loving someone was too painful and she didn't want Adam to ever experience what she had.

When she walked into the living room Adam had turned on his game console and was showing George some kind of apocalyptic zombie war game he was into.

George was standing there and watching it.

"Did you make your call?" she asked.

George glanced back at her. "Yeah, there are a lot of calls tonight so it's going to take about twenty minutes before they can get a cab for me. I can wait outside."

"No, you can stay here. Maybe play a round with me?" Adam said, with hope in his voice.

George raised his eyebrows in question at her.

"Sure, he can play a quick round." What else was she going to say? No. Get out. Leave my son alone. "Are you sure George wants to play your gun game?"

"Zombie Moon Apocalypse Four? Sure, I like

that game." George sat down on the couch and Adam handed him a control.

"You know the name of the game?" Samantha asked in amazement.

George shrugged as he fell right into gameplay with Adam. "Oh, yeah, not much to do sometimes in the winter. I have several of these... Watch the guy on your back!"

"Got him!" Adam fired off something that made a horrible laser sound. "Good shot, George."

"Not bad yourself."

Samantha watched in amazement.

"Mom *hates* these games. When she tries to play she's eaten within the first minute." Adam was grinning as he continued hacking zombies into small pieces.

George grinned and stole a glance at her. "I'm sure she'd be fine with some practice."

Adam snorted at the same time she did.

"I have no interest in blowing up zombies," Samantha said.

"Come on, Doxtator. It's saving the world." George winked at her and returned to the game.

Fifteen minutes and numerous zombie deaths later, George glanced at the clock. "Sorry, buddy, I'm going to have to head outside. My cab should be here soon. Thanks for letting me play, though. I haven't met many people down here who like to game and it gets boring on your own."

"Aw." Adam shut the game down. "Do you have to go?"

"Yes," Samantha said, standing up. "Mr. Atavik has to get up for work tomorrow."

George cocked an eyebrow. "Mr. Atavik?"

"That's your name."

"No, that's my father's name. I'm George."

Adam stood up and fist-bumped George. "I hope you come by again. I'd love to play some other games with you."

"It was fun," George said, returning the fist-bump but thankfully not promising that he'd see Adam again.

You're being ridiculous.

She couldn't play these games with Adam and Joyce's words were ringing in her ears once again, the part about a father figure.

"Maybe George can come back one day when he has some time off."

George looked her with surprise and then cleared his throat. "Yeah, maybe."

Samantha led him to the door. "Thanks again for making sure I got home."

George opened the door. "No problem. I'll see you tomorrow."

Samantha watched George walk down the hallway and out the front doors. She shut her door and locked it. Adam was leaning against the couch.

"He's pretty cool," Adam announced.

Samantha cocked an eyebrow. "Oh, yes?"

"Yeah, I hope he comes around again."

"Adam, he's training and he probably doesn't have time."

Adam looked disappointed. "Too bad. He's a good gamer."

She nodded. "Why don't you get ready for bed? It's late."

"Aw, do I have to?"

"Yes."

With much protest Adam headed down the hall to the bathroom and she let out a sigh of relief and relaxed against the door.

She was being ridiculous. George could be her friend. She had lots of friends.

I don't have lots of guy friends.

Still, maybe she could give Adam a male influence, even for a short while, because when it came to George, all it could ever be was a short while.

CHAPTER SEVEN

WHEN GEORGE CAME out of a mandatory training class, he saw Samantha across the room. She was sitting at her desk, bent over some paperwork, and as if sensing his gaze she looked up from her desk and George's pulse began to race.

Things had been a little tense since yesterday when he'd been at her apartment. Not that being at her apartment meant anything, far from it, but he'd met her son and in the brief time he'd hung out with Adam he'd actually enjoyed their time together. He wished he could have spent still more time with Samantha and Adam, but that was a big no-no.

Being around Samantha was proving to be difficult, because the more he tried to keep himself from getting closer, the more he was drawn to her. He just couldn't help himself. He was ruled by the instincts of desire.

It had been a tough night for him. Not only because he was hadn't been able to get Samantha from his thoughts, but he'd learned a close friend of his was getting married.

He was happy for the guy, but for the first time in a while he was envious.

He'd asked Cheryl and she'd said yes. Then, before he'd known it, it had all been over. He hadn't even had a chance to buy her a ring. He'd planned this whole elaborate set-up in Cape Recluse at her place. He'd brought in chocolates from the city and non-alcoholic champagne.

Then the crash had happened and all those well-intentioned plans had crumbled away.

There had been no congratulations for them.

Only sympathy for him, which had made him angry.

All he had wanted was to be left alone so he could mend the pieces of his shattered heart. He hadn't needed sympathy. He hadn't wanted it.

George stood in front of her desk. "What's on the agenda today?"

"Nothing much." Samantha set down her

paperwork. "You might as well study while you can for your test."

"Sounds good." Only he didn't move away. "Any plans for the weekend?"

He tried not to wince; he hated making small talk.

"No. How about you?"

"I'll probably spend the weekend watching Clint Eastwood movies or something. I don't know many people in the city."

Samantha bit her lip, she seemed to be hesitating. "Look, why don't you come over to my place on Saturday for dinner?"

George had to make sure his mouth didn't drop to the floor he was so shocked by the question. He would love to go to her place for dinner, but he wasn't sure if that was the smartest course of action. Maybe he hadn't heard her correctly. "What?"

"I know I'm your mentor and everything, but can't we be friends?"

"Sure, I thought we kind of were," George said.

Friends. Yeah, he could be friends with her. He was positive he could.

Then Samantha blushed and she tucked a strand of her dark hair behind her ear. He fought back the urge to reach out and touch it, to see if it was as silky soft as he thought it was.

"Of—of course we are. Look, do you want to come over for dinner or not?"

No. Say no.

Only he couldn't. He was weak.

"Sure. What time?"

"Around four?"

"You eat like a senior citizen," George teased.

She rolled her eyes. "I don't eat *that* early, but I thought you might want to come over and finish off a certain zombie exploding game you started."

"Ah, yes. Sure, I can come over at four. Do you want me to bring anything?"

Samantha shook her head and picked up her bag. "No, just yourself."

George watched her leave and head to the locker room.

What the heck had just happened?

He'd told himself just a few moments ago that he was going to keep his distance, to keep it professional, and once again he'd found himself drawn in.

Helpless.

He could do this. They could just be friends and it would be nice not to spend another weekend alone in his apartment, watching the same movies over and over and missing home.

He missed his family and he missed flying most of all. He had to get out there and make more friends, but for now he'd hang out at Samantha's. There was nothing wrong with being her friend.

He had lots of girlfriends.

Okay, that was a lie. All of his friends who were of the female persuasion were his sisters.

If his grandmother were alive now she'd be hitting him upside of the head and telling him he had a right to move on after Cheryl. To not let the ghosts of the past haunt his present life. Which was true.

George ran his fingers through his hair and picked up his book bag from the table and followed in Samantha's footsteps to the locker room. He didn't get more than three paces before the sirens went off and she came running out.

"Look alive, Atavik," she shouted.

"What's going on?"

"An accident just north of the city," Samantha said, running past him. "Hop to it."

George set down his knapsack and ran after her.

He'd worry about his personal problems later. Right now he had a job to do.

"No stupid heroics this time," Samantha teased George as she slowed the ambulance.

"No promises." He winked at her and she tried not to laugh.

She took a deep breath and looked out the window. The accident didn't look too bad, well, not as bad as the accident of a couple of days ago, when George had run toward the flames to save that child.

She glanced at his arm. It wasn't bandaged any longer. The burn looked dark and seemed to be healing over. Which was good.

She still couldn't believe he'd done that.

"Here we are," she said.

"Should I stick close?" he asked.

"No need. Come on." Samantha pushed open the door and jumped outside, with George following close behind her. They reached in through the open back doors and pulled out the stretcher.

They headed toward the first car, where the firefighters were using the jaws of life to prise open the mangled remains.

"Let's go." She took a deep breath and pushed the gurney forward. "What do we have here?"

"Lone female, seat belt and air bag deployed. She was unconscious on our arrival, but she appears to be conscious at the moment."

Samantha carefully made her way to the side of the car, where the door had been prised away.

A firefighter stood by ready to cut the seat belt away once Samantha had examined the victim.

"Ma'am, my name is Samantha. Can you hear me?"

"What?" The words were slurred and the woman didn't raise her head.

Samantha leaned in closer and gently placed her gloved hand on the woman's forehead to get a closer look. "Ma'am, can you tell me your name?"

"What?"

"Looks like a probable concussion. Bring me the back brace, George, and we'll get her ready to transport."

George nodded and pulled the brace off the gurney. He set it down and climbed in on the other side of the woman.

"Ready when you are, Lieutenant."

The firefighter nodded and stepped forward to cut the seat belt and George and Samantha braced themselves to stabilize the injured woman.

"On my count, one, two, three."

The firefighter cut away the seat belt and the woman cried out as George and Samantha gently got her down on the back brace and strapped her down.

She whimpered a bit but didn't fight them.

They lifted her up and got the back brace stabilized on the gurney. Samantha leaned over the woman and gently pried open her eyelids, shining a light into her eyes. "Pupils are reactive, but one is dilated."

"What?" The woman slurred again.

"Ma'am, do you know where you are?"

The woman didn't answer, but her eyes rolled back in her head.

"Found her identification in her purse," George said.

"Good. We'll take it to the hospital."

"There's bleeding. Perhaps a depressed skull fracture?" George asked.

"Let's get her out of here."

They rolled the stretcher to the ambulance and loaded the woman up. George secured the gurney and Samantha closed the doors. George then started preparing the patient's arm to get an IV hooked up, while Samantha secured an oxygen mask over her face. Once everything was dealt with and the doors secured, she jumped out and climbed into the driver's seat.

"Hang onto your hat!" Samantha started the engine and flicked on the siren and lights.

George took the seat next to the stretcher, watching the woman's blood pressure on the monitor.

"How's the patient?" Samantha called out over her shoulder.

"Stable, but it'll be good when we get her to the hospital. Her GCS is three."

"Yeah, we'll be there soon."

Samantha kept her focus on the road in front of the ambulance, watching as cars pulled over to the side to let them through.

In a matter of minutes she was pulling up in front of the emergency department at the hospital. Samantha leapt into action as they moved gear and got the stretcher ready to transport.

She opened the back door and George jumped

down beside her as they worked together to get the patient out of the ambulance. Once the stretcher was level George secured the bolus bag and the oxygen tank and they wheeled the patient inside. George carried her identification.

"Patient is Irene Johnstone. She's a fifty-three-year-old female who was the lone, belted occupant in a double car collision. Air bag was deployed," Samantha's voice sounded over the emergency room din as a trauma doctor came out of an alcove and helped George and her guide the patient into a trauma pod.

"Left pupil is dilated and she had a GCS score of three in the field," Samantha said.

"Let's get a portable X-ray in here, *stat*!" the doctor shouted.

She handed over the information to the nurses as George helped an intern and some nurses transfer the patient onto a hospital stretcher. They waited as the doctor slipped her off the back brace.

Once George had retrieved the back brace

they pushed the stretcher out of trauma pod and let the doctors take over.

"That was a rush. I think that was the fastest transfer I've ever been in down here," George said, as he set the back brace down on the stretcher.

"Well, things can move a bit faster when you're not waiting for a plane."

"True." George pushed the stretcher out of the emergency exit doors toward the ambulance. "Still, in my experience, things did move pretty quickly on a plane."

Samantha perked up. She wasn't going to badger him about his flight experience, but if he was willing to talk she was going to listen. "Oh, yes?"

"Yeah, well, when the nearest hospital is only accessible by air and you have a life-threatening…" He trailed off and opened the ambulance doors to return the stretcher.

She wanted to know what it was that was affecting him so much, but that wasn't any of her business.

You wanted to keep this professional.

"Did you know that it's Victoria Day this weekend?" Her cheeks flushed because that was probably the dumbest tension breaker she'd ever used.

George's brow furrowed. "Really? Yeah, you're right. I completely forgot. Do you want to postpone dinner?"

"No, not at all. I just forgot it was a long weekend. It just occurred to me. Not that it matters since we work Monday."

George grinned, his eyes twinkling and so like himself again. "No rest for the wicked, eh?"

Samantha was going to answer when a call came through on the radio.

"Doxtator, Ambulance 3326," she answered.

"Ambulance 3326, you're wanted at building E of the hospital. Patient transfer to Stratford."

"Roger that. Ambulance 3326 responding." Samantha hung up the receiver.

"What was that?" George asked.

"There's a patient transport on the other side of the hospital. Dispatch asked us to take it since we're here. Let's go." She climbed in the front. George was already seated there.

"How far is it to Stratford from here?"

"About an hour with traffic."

George nodded. "This is also what I like about a land ambulance, I get to sit back and enjoy the sights."

"You could drive, you know, Atavik. You've got to learn the ins and outs of driving the ambulance some time," Samantha said.

"Really?"

George glanced at her and she shrugged her shoulders. "Sure. It's just a simple patient transfer."

"Sounds good."

They traded spots and he took the wheel and started the engine.

"You're doing great. Just ease it on out and flash the lights." Samantha pointed at the switch, reminding him where it was. George flipped it and guided the ambulance out of the emergency bay.

"Just lead the way, boss."

"Take the first right at the end and we'll follow it to Building E."

"Gotcha."

George handled the ambulance with ease. He didn't really need this course, not to learn anything. He just needed the legal certification, but Samantha felt like she was working with an equal. This wasn't a teacher–student relationship.

This was a partner. She liked having George nearby to chat to, even if it was just about work. It was adult conversation and Samantha realized how she'd missed this.

She'd forgotten how lonely she was.

CHAPTER EIGHT

I FORGOT TO ask him what he likes to eat! I hope he likes what I've made.

She shook her head, angry at herself for second-guessing what she made. It was good enough. She'd just invited George over for a friendly barbecue. That's it.

Adam was bouncing around, excited because he was looking forward to spending mind-numbing hours playing video games with George.

Samantha was happy that he was so excited.

She had no reason to stress out or be nervous. This was just a dinner between friends, between coworkers.

Except she didn't think of George in the same way as her other coworkers. None of the others gave her a heady rush when they shared a look. *Stop that. He's just a friend.* Of course, she and Cameron had started out as friends.

Cameron had been her best friend. She missed coming home and talking to someone, an adult.

Adam was great, but it was different. There were things she couldn't share with him or talk to him about. And she was sure there were things Adam wanted to talk to a man about.

She glanced over at Adam. There wasn't much of Cameron in him. Adam had the same dark hair as she did, the same skin tone and eyes. The only part of Cameron there was the dimples and the smile.

Maybe once she was settled up north she'd try to date, but even that thought left her feeling unsatisfied because the person she was most interested in was taboo.

No matter how many times she told herself there was no future between her and George, whenever she thought about getting into the dating scene again she always thought of him.

And it had to stop.

The buzzer went off, snapping her out of the familiar thoughts that seemed to cycle through her brain over and over again.

Taking a deep breath to calm her suddenly jittery nerves, she pushed the buzzer on the wall. "Hello?"

"It's George."

"Come on in." She pushed the unlock button and released the intercom.

"Yes! It's awesome he's here. This is going to be fun." Adam was jumping up and down with excitement again and Samantha chuckled at his enthusiasm.

"He may not want to be monopolized by you the entire time, Adam. He may like video games, but—"

"Yeah, I know, he's an adult." Adam shrugged. "It'll be awesome anyway."

George knocked on the door and Adam bolted past her to open it. "Hey, George."

"Hey, Adam, got the controllers warmed up for me?"

Oh, lord. Samantha just shook her head.

Then moved over so she could see through to the entranceway and her breath caught in her throat at the sight of George in his everyday clothes.

Dammit, he was just as handsome as ever. He was wearing dark brown jeans and a navy blue long-sleeved V-neck top with a white shirt underneath and a brown suede jacket. Adam was talking his ear off and George was smiling that large bright smile at him, genuinely interested in what he had to say.

In his hand was a paper bag from the liquor store.

"I thought you didn't drink?" she said, stepping between Adam and George to take the paper bag from him.

"I don't, but my grandmother always said when you're invited over to someone's house for the first time you bring something. I didn't know what else to bring so Lizzie told me what your favorite brand of wine was." Then he grinned and chuckled. "Though I had a heck of a time asking for it."

Adam, bored with the conversation, ran into

the living room, leaving Samantha and George standing there.

George pulled off his jacket and Samantha took it with her free hand.

"I think she thought I was a special individual. Stupid northerners." He winked.

"More like teetotalers. Thanks for the wine, by the way. Just head into the living room. Adam has been eagerly awaiting your arrival."

George chuckled. "Has he?" He ran his fingers through his hair. "I'll head there in a moment. Is there anything I can help you with?"

Samantha placed the wine bottle on the dining-room table and then hung up his coat in the closet. "No, I don't think so. I hope you don't mind steaks."

"Why would I mind steaks? That sounds great."

She smiled. "Oh, good. I'd forgotten to ask you what you like to eat."

"Seriously, steaks are great. The only thing I'm allergic to is kiwi."

"Damn, my steaks are slathered in kiwi. Just

teasing. Go on into the other room and I'll fire up the barbecue."

"Hey, do you mind if I grill them?"

"You're my guest," she protested.

George shrugged. "I don't have a barbecue down here. It's kind of a Victoria Day tradition for me."

"What about Adam?"

"He can hang outside with me." George went into the living room. "Yo, Adam, I'm going to grill the steaks for your mom. Want to hang outside with me?"

Samantha steeled herself for his disappointment, but was surprised when she heard Adam agree enthusiastically.

George came back. "Looks like it's all set. Where's your lighter?"

She reached into a drawer and pulled out the slim red lighter. "Here you go. You really don't have to do this. You're my guest."

"Don't worry about it. This way it'll really feel like Victoria Day. The only difference is I won't have my sisters nagging at me that I'm doing it wrong or I'm going to burn stuff."

Samantha grimaced. "Don't tell me you burn stuff."

"No, I don't." George winked again, which didn't make her feel at ease. She followed him into the living room. "Show me where this barbecue is, Adam."

"Out the sliding doors." Adam pulled the blinds and unlocked the sliding doors, jumping out onto the patio.

George followed. "Hey, you guys have a pool. Sweet."

"It's a shared pool," Adam responded. "It's pretty cool. Want to kick a ball around?"

Samantha wandered over to watch them through the dining-room window and was amazed at how quickly Adam was falling in with George, but she could see the appeal. He was like a big kid most of the time and the thought frightened her. She didn't want Adam to get hurt.

George finished lighting the grill and then

headed out onto the green space where Adam was and began to kick the ball around with him.

Samantha smiled. It was hard not to watch Adam enjoy time with George.

She was in serious trouble, but at this moment she wasn't sure if she really wanted to run or not.

While George was grilling the steaks Samantha set up her little patio set and chairs. She'd planned to have the dinner inside in the dining room, but the sun was shining and it wasn't too hot outside. It was a nice evening.

Even Adam was impressed.

"We never eat outside. Awesome!"

George laughed. "Never? That seems a shame. It's nice out here. No threat of a polar bear wandering in and eating you."

Adam's eyes widened. "Does that happen?"

George shook his head. "No, we have to be mindful of them, but my hometown is a pretty big settlement they keep out of for the most part."

"Holy cow."

Samantha spread the tablecloth. "I guess I never really thought about bears as being an everyday occurrence."

"They're not an everyday occurrence, but from a young age we're warned about their presence. I mean, it's eat or be eaten up there." Then he laughed to himself at some private joke.

"What's so funny?"

"Something my sister Charlotte said to her husband when they were talking about the same thing. He still gets pretty pale in the face when you mention polar bears."

"Have you ever had any close calls?" Adam asked, totally riveted.

"Sure," George said offhandedly, like it was an everyday thing. "But I know how to use a high-powered rifle."

"Whoa." Adam's mouth dropped open. "Where do you live again?"

George gave him a funny look. "London."

Samantha laughed as Adam rolled his eyes. "I mean where did you grow up, obviously."

"Cape Recluse in Nunavut. It's near the national park."

"Cool," Adam said.

"It can be, or so I'm told," Samantha teased, as he began to set the table. She caught George's gaze and they shared a smile, which made her pulse quicken and butterflies in her stomach began to flutter like she was some kind of giddy schoolgirl.

"What's around your neck?" Adam asked, stepping a bit closer. "It looks like a bear."

"It's my totem. It is a bear. What's your totem?"

Adam shrugged. "I don't have a totem."

George grinned. "Well, maybe your spirit guide will speak to you soon and you'll find out your totem."

Curious, Samantha moved closer and saw he wore a leather necklace with a white carved bear that rested at the base of his throat.

Bears meant strength, confidence, but their medicine could mean healing. It had been a long time since she'd thought about something from her heritage, because that was not the way her mother had raised them. Which seemed odd to her now, because her mother was full-Ojibway and had grown up just outside a reserve.

Her mother had raised her and her siblings more from her father's side.

When she'd been younger she'd always wanted to learn more, to preserve her heritage, but then she'd met Cameron and they'd gone to college to become paramedics and her good intentions had fallen by the wayside.

Her son knew very little about their heritage and she felt a bit guilty for not teaching him more. Maybe that's why he was connecting with George. He saw something in him he could identify with.

Adam attended a school where the population was very multicultural, but when you were the only First Nation boy in class, she could see why Adam was so interested.

At least when they moved up to Thunder Bay when she took the job with the air crew, they would be closer to some of her family and maybe he could learn a bit more about his family culture. And he'd have plenty of cousins to play with as two of her sisters and her mother lived out there.

"It's beautiful. What's it carved out of?" she asked.

"Whalebone. My grandmother carved it when I was born." George touched it and got that wistful look on his face. One she knew all too well. It was the look when you missed someone who was gone.

"You never did tell me her name so I could look her up."

"Anernerk Kamut."

Samantha's eyes widened. "I *have* heard of her. That's the one Inuit artist I'm aware of. I had no idea you were her grandson!"

George laughed. "One of many. She had fifteen kids."

Samantha's mouth dropped open. "So Cape Recluse really is populated by most of your family."

"We didn't all stay there. Case in point." He

turned back to the steaks. "These are almost done. Can I get a clean plate to put these on?"

"Sure. Adam, run inside and bring a clean plate."

"Okay," Adam moaned, dragging himself inside.

"I'd better get the sides. I hope you like potato salad and garden salad."

"Sounds good." George turned back to grilling and Samantha headed inside to get the rest of the stuff for dinner.

When she came outside with the last salad and a pitcher of iced tea George was dishing out the steaks and Adam was seated between them, his fork and his knife in his hands.

"You have one ravenous beast here," George said, nodding toward Adam.

"Yes, apparently he's forgotten the manners I've taught him."

Adam blushed and set down his fork and knife.

When George took his seat, Samantha sat down and they dished out the salads.

"This looks great, I haven't had a home-cooked meal in a while. Thanks for having me over, Sam."

"You're welcome." Samantha could feel the heat of a blush in her cheeks again as she poured some iced tea into his glass.

"Maybe there'll be some fireworks tonight!" Adam said.

Samantha's hand shook and she spilled some iced tea on George's hand. "I'm sorry."

George's dark eyes were twinkling. "Do they set them off on the Saturday before Victoria Day?"

Adam nodded. "Sometimes, though Mom usually works on Victoria Day and can't take me to the park to watch the city display. Luckily Grandma and Grandpa take me. It's really cool."

Adam continued eating.

"It's going to be hard on them when you guys move north," George said. "I know when one of my aunts or uncles moved away it was hard on Grandma to be away from her grandkids. Even if she did clip us around the head all the time." George winked at Adam.

"Yeah, it will be, but they understand why I'm doing it. It was Cameron's and my plan all along. He loved the north just as much as me."

George nodded. "It's a shame sometimes how families can become so spread out, but at least you can video chat or something."

"Do you do that with your family up north?" Samantha asked.

"I have to or my sisters would murder me."

She chuckled. "Yes, I video chat with my sisters in Thunder Bay regularly."

"You have family in Thunder Bay?"

Samantha nodded. "Yes, or I might not be as brave about moving us up there to live."

They enjoyed pleasant conversation and a great dinner out on her patio. When dinner was over Adam cleared the table under threat that he might not get his allowance if he didn't, and George and Samantha sat in the chairs, watching the sun go down.

"Adam hasn't complained once that you two haven't spent any time blowing stuff up."

George chuckled. "We all need time away

from the computer. Thanks again for having me over."

"You're welcome. I just felt bad that you had no plans and you were on your own."

He winked. "You mean you felt bad I was alone."

Samantha chuckled. "I didn't say alone."

"Isn't on your own and alone the same?"

"Perhaps, but I think alone sounds more sad. Like, aw, he's all alone." She made a pouty face and he laughed. "I don't like being classified as alone."

He cocked his head to one side. "Yeah, it sucks. The pity."

She wanted to ask him how he could commiserate. He wasn't a widower. His file didn't state anything about him having been married before. There was no big D on his file or a big W like there was on hers.

"Well, I'm usually alone," George said nervously, clearly uncomfortable with the silence. "I'm not *that* social."

"I find that hard to believe," she said.

"Why?"

"You made fast friends with a lot of emergency workers that first day on the job."

"Being friendly and having friends are different things. I don't have a lot of friends. Only a couple good ones and they're mostly family. I guess I'm just weird."

"I don't think you're weird," Samantha said.

George raised an eyebrow. "Oh, really? What if I told you about my obsessive love for Clint Eastwood?"

"Obsessive love? Okay, that might be a little weird."

"Well, maybe love isn't the right word I'm looking for. I like his movies. All his movies, but especially the westerns."

"Really?" she asked in fascination. "I never took you for a Dirty Harry type of guy."

"Dirty Harry wasn't a cowboy. He was a cop."

Samantha snorted. "Same guy."

"What? How is a cowboy in the old west the same as a cop in the seventies?"

"I'm afraid I'm not a Clint Eastwood fan. I prefer John Wayne."

George's mouth fell open. "Okay, now, *that's* surprising. You like John Wayne."

Samantha rolled her eyes. "I don't mind John Wayne. I'd watch a John Wayne movie over a Clint Eastwood movie any day. I prefer musicals like *Oklahoma!*."

George wrinkled is nose. "Yuck, just like my sisters. Well, what about *Paint Your Wagon*? That was a musical and it featured Clint Eastwood."

"Never heard of that one." Samantha took a sip of her iced tea. "You'll have to show it to me one day."

What am I doing?

"Deal," George responded, not noticing how her cheeks were flaming, but then again the sun was setting into twilight.

"Not so fast. It's not a done deal yet. You have to watch a musical of my choosing if you're going to subject me to a Clint Eastwood musical."

George rolled his eyes. "Oh, the torture."

"Tough. Those are the terms."

"Fine," George said. He pretended to be grumpy, but he was smiling to himself. "It's really a nice night. Kind of sucks we don't get the long weekend. I wouldn't mind seeing what kind of firework display the city puts on."

"Yeah, but that's one of our mandatory night shifts. You might see some if it's slow. Dispatch is close to the conservation area and they always put on a firework show there too."

"A slow night wouldn't be a bad thing."

Samantha nodded in agreement. A slow night would mean that no one was sick or injured and that was always a good thing. The only downside to a slow night was that it dragged on and on.

Usually one of the others on duty would break out the cards and they'd have a game of euchre and somehow avoid the game of strip poker that someone *always* suggested.

"So you've heard of my grandmother? How

random that the one Inuit artist you're familiar with is her."

"My father had one of her pieces. He spent some time up in Nunavut before it was Nunavut, when it was still a part of Northwest Territories and Iqaluit was Frobisher Bay."

George looked surprised. "Oh, yes? What did he do up there?"

"He was an RCMP officer."

George whistled. "Royal Canadian Mounted Police. That's impressive. How did your parents meet?"

"He got stationed to the office in the town where my mother worked as a border guard at the one small ferry crossing there."

"How random."

"Aren't meetings usually random? Look at us, for example. Totally random."

"Are they?" He leaned closer. "I guess they are. How did you and your late husband meet?"

Samantha sighed. "Through mutual friends. I went to school on the reservation and he was from a town nearby. Our friends happened to be dating and we just met, but, yeah, I guess it was totally random."

George grinned. "Maybe it was predestined."

"Maybe. Not sure if I believe in destiny."

"That's too bad." He took a sip of his iced tea. "So are your friends still together?"

"No. They're not." She ran her fingers around the stem of her wineglass. "So, what about you?"

He shrugged. "What about me?"

"Any significant other?"

The expression on George's face hardened. "I was engaged once."

"What happened?" she asked.

"It didn't work out." He looked away and then back at her quickly. "So, yeah, I get despairing of the pity others give you. I don't like it. I don't want it."

"I wasn't going to give you any."

Their gaze locked across the table, even though it was twilight and he was half-obscured in shadows, she could see the sparkle in his eyes. The one that made her feel weak at the knees.

Her heart beat a bit faster as George leaned

closer to her. She fought the urge to reach across and kiss him. She wanted to kiss him.

Her whole body was shouting at her to do just that.

There was a loud crack and a wailing whistle.

"Fireworks," George said, but still looked at her.

"What?"

Then he turned and pointed. "Fireworks."

Adam came rushing outside. "I heard fireworks. Yes!" He high fived George and then sat down at her feet, leaning against her.

"I thought they weren't allowed to set fireworks off in their backyard."

"They can, on this weekend after dusk."

Adam grinned up at the two of them. "This is great."

Samantha glanced at George, who was smiling at them, a smile that warmed her to her very core. Samantha didn't answer anything. She just ran her fingers through her son's hair and thought that, yeah, it was pretty great.

CHAPTER NINE

WHEN GEORGE GOT back home from Samantha's home his apartment looked really empty. It was pretty sparse to begin with, bachelor living at its finest, and he'd lived that way in Cape Recluse, but it had never bothered him before.

Until now.

Now his apartment was empty and hollow.

It made him realize just how lonely he actually was.

He could really settle down with a woman like Samantha. Except he wasn't sure he could open his heart again.

"You're a stubborn ox!" He could hear his grandmother's voice in his head. She'd often referred to him as a stubborn ox.

With a heavy sigh he pulled off his jacket and tossed it on a nearby chair. He headed to his futon, which served as his couch and his bed. He sat down and stared at the blank television.

It's okay to love again.

But Samantha had made it clear that she was just being a good friend to a lonely coworker.

Nothing more.

He didn't blame her for not wanting to get involved with just anyone. She had a kid. A great kid, who was a little obsessed with blowing up zombies but a good kid none the less.

George smiled as he thought about playing that game with Adam after the short firework show had ended.

He'd stayed at Samantha's until Adam went to bed.

When Samantha had said goodnight he'd fought the urge to reach out and take her in his arms. He'd wanted to run his hands through her ebony hair and press those soft lips against his. He wanted her. He thought about it constantly and it made him feel bad.

You can't have her.

Samantha had never shown him anything

other than friendship, and he wasn't the kind of guy to pester her for a date. Only he knew Samantha felt the same way. She just wasn't the type of woman who would get together with someone for a temporary fling. She had a son to think of.

He got it. He respected it. And he couldn't promise forever. With the state his heart was in, how could he promise anything?

He ran his fingers through his hair and picked up the remote, starting the last Clint Eastwood movie he'd been watching, but after a few minutes he realized he wasn't paying attention. He really needed to get to bed.

Not that he had any exciting plans for tomorrow.

His phone rang, which was odd.

"Hello?"

"Hi, George, it's Sam."

"Samantha? Did I forget something?"

"No, no... I was wondering...I was wondering if you'd like to take a trip with Adam and me to the beach tomorrow. It's supposed to be a hot day."

Say no. Only he couldn't.

"Sure. I'm not doing anything."

"Great." There was relief in her voice. "Adam wanted to invite you."

"Just Adam?"

"Y-yes. Adam."

George smiled to himself because he'd heard the nervousness in her voice and though he shouldn't go, he couldn't help himself. What else was he going to do tomorrow?

"Okay. What time should I swing by your place?"

"I'll pick you up tomorrow about ten. We'll have lunch."

"Should I pack my swimming trunks?" he teased.

She laughed. "It's still not warm enough but, hey, if it floats your boat."

"Ten sounds great."

"We'll just hang out on the sand, play catch."

He rattled off his address when she asked for

it and told her he'd meet her downstairs at ten. They said goodbye and he hung up the phone.

George scrubbed his hands over his face. What had just happened? He told himself he wasn't going to pursue her. He should keep it professional, but he was like a moth to her flame. He wanted to spend time with her.

We're friends. Nothing more.

Friends could hang out at the beach. Friends did stuff like that. Just because he was attracted to her it didn't mean it had to be anything more. Only being around Samantha made him forget the pain that still scarred his soul. A pain she understood too.

He didn't think about the accident or Cheryl so much when he was around Samantha. She made the pain of it all disappear, which was another reason why he was so drawn to her.

Stop thinking about it.

He had to get a grip on himself. He had to stop thinking about Samantha as more than a friend, only he knew that was going to be impossible.

I should call her and cancel. He picked up his phone, only to set it down again.

He couldn't cancel. If he did that it would disappoint Adam and he didn't want to hurt Adam, so he'd go, but then he wouldn't say yes to any more outings with her unless it was work related. It had to end now.

He got undressed and decided to take a nice cold shower.

Maybe that would clear his mind. He turned on the shower and stepped under the spray, and tried to let his mind go blank. He tried to think about anything else, but in spite of his best efforts he couldn't get Samantha or the desire he felt for her out of his brain.

He'd said it before, he was a doomed man.

He was exhausted. George stifled back a yawn as he waited for Samantha and Adam outside his apartment. He'd tossed and turned all night, thinking about Cheryl and what she'd done to him.

He came to the conclusion, like he always did,

that he and Samantha would just be friends and he had to be more guarded with his emotions, especially with his overwhelming desire for her, and that was going to be a hard thing to keep under wraps.

George didn't want a relationship. Not now when his life was in upheaval, and he especially didn't want a relationship with a pilot.

Always worried about her up in the sky.

Of course, all his good intentions went flying out the window the moment her silver minivan pulled into the loop in front of his building.

The window on the passenger side rolled down and George peered in.

"I thought minivans were for soccer moms?" he teased.

"It's a good vehicle to have, especially as I'm moving north. I can haul a lot with it."

George grinned. He loved the way she thought, so like him.

No. Don't get sucked in.

He tried to rein in the naughty side of him, the side that wanted her so badly, but it was hard when she looked so darned beautiful, so laid-back and relaxed in capri pants and a summery blouse with her hair down around her shoulders.

He was a lost man. This was going to be more challenging than he'd thought.

Turn around. Walk away, it's your only hope.

Only he ignored the thought that told him to run and climbed in the passenger side.

"Hey, Adam." George glanced over to see Adam with his face almost pressed against a portable gaming system.

"Hi," Adam responded, but was still focused on his game.

"Are you sure this was Adam's idea?" George teased.

"Oh, yeah, he just hates the long drive. Especially through the city. This city needs a bypass road to avoid the congestion going north-south."

George nodded. "Agreed. It took me ages yesterday to get from one end to the other. The traffic was thick."

"At least it's not as bad as Toronto."

"I'd never drive there." George shuddered. "Too many people."

Samantha frowned. "Do crowds bother you that much?"

"A bit. I'm not scared of them or anything. I'm just not *used* to them."

"You might not enjoy Grand Bend, then."

George's brow creased. "Why do you say that?"

"Come the long weekend or the summer it's always jam-packed, but it's a great beach."

George leaned back and looked out the window. He thought if he focused on the sights, maybe he could fight the need to reach over and touch her.

The countryside north of London was pretty with lots of farmland. Young crops were peeking up through the dark soil. He wasn't used to the sight of acres and acres of fields. Nunavut wasn't suitable for farming like this.

After about an hour of going west they hit highway twenty-one and the farmland gave way to the tall pine forests that grew along the southern shore of Lake Huron. It was beautiful. The only thing that took away from what would be a tranquil ride through a forest was the steady flow of traffic as they headed north into Grand Bend.

"It's pretty busy," Samantha remarked.

"I can see that."

"Sorry," Samantha said, as she turned into the overflowing beach parking lot.

"Why are you apologizing? Did you summon the crowd here?"

"Well, no." Pink stained her cheeks. "It's just a lot nicer when hardly anyone is around."

"So, like in winter?"

They both laughed. It was easy to laugh with her.

Samantha found a parking spot and they got out. George grabbed the beach chairs, Samantha grabbed the picnic basket and Adam the umbrella.

The sand seeped in through cracks in George's sneakers.

"You should've worn thongs."

George froze. "What did you say?"

Samantha chuckled and held out her foot. "You know, sandals, flip-flops."

"Oh, yeah. I thought you told me to wear a thong and I was picturing, you know, a thong."

Adam wrinkled his nose. "Dude, that's gross."

"Why do think I was so horrified?" George said.

They found a spot near some tall trees off to the side of the main beach. George popped open the chairs while Samantha set up the umbrella and Adam laid out the blanket.

There was a nice breeze coming off the lake, which took some of the sizzle out of the bright sun.

George sat down and looked up and down the beach. It was pretty busy. There were a lot of young people and he could see several games of beach volleyball and some kites in the air.

"Mom, can I fly my kite?" Adam asked, pulling out a collapsible one from his knapsack.

"Sure, but stay where I can see you."

Adam nodded and ran closer to the water to get his kite airborne.

Samantha let out a sigh. "I love being at the beach."

"I can see why," George said. "It's wonderful, the water and the sand. This is what I like about living down here. I wonder how cold the water is?"

Samantha grinned. "Cold, but, hey, you might feel right at home."

There was a sparkle of devilment in her eyes and he couldn't help but laugh.

Damn.

He was falling fast, he could feel it and it scared him.

I don't deserve this.

He wasn't ready for a relationship, especially one with such an uncertain future.

"So why do you like this beach so much? I mean, of all the beaches there are in Ontario, why this particular beach?"

Samantha looked confused. "What an odd question."

"Are you surprised? I mean, I have talked about weird things before, or do I need to remind you about taxi turkey?"

"Please don't."

"So, why this place?"

Samantha shrugged. "I had my wedding not far from here and the pictures done here."

George could hear the sadness in her voice. He hated hearing her so wistful. He understood that. She had a broken heart. At least her husband had loved her until the end. That was something to be grateful for.

"How did he die?"

Samantha's head dropped and she stared at her hands in her lap. "A brain tumor."

"I'm sorry."

She smiled. "Thanks. There was nothing they could do at that point. It was inoperable. Adam was only a baby."

George glanced at Adam, who was running along the beach, and he felt a pang of pain for him. He was sorry that Adam hadn't got to know his father or that his father hadn't known what a great son he'd had.

"Doesn't it hurt, coming back here?" George asked, because he hadn't been able to return to the few places he had memories of sharing with Cheryl. It stung too much to be where they'd laughed or made love. It just reminded him of what an idiot he'd been.

"No." Samantha sighed and tucked a flyaway strand of hair behind her ear. "It was hard at first but, no, it doesn't bother me, coming back to where we shared memories. It helped me move on, actually."

"How?"

Samantha chuckled. "I don't know, maybe because it just reminds me of him. I carry a piece of him with me always, and if I think about the good times it lessens the pain. You know?"

Only he didn't know, because his pain was similar, but so different than hers. They'd both had a broken heart at one point in their lives, but hers was pure. His was tainted.

Samantha sighed. "Like I said, Cameron loved the beach. So do I."

"That's a nice memory to have of him." He wanted to reach out and take her in his arms, to hold her, but he didn't.

"Since we're talking about beaches, where's your favorite beach?"

George leaned over. "Mexico."

They laughed at that. Every time he spent time with her he laughed and enjoyed himself. He forgot about the plane crash, he forgot he'd lost his best friend.

He forgot about a lot of things.

Including the fact he only wanted to stay friends with Samantha, but it was so hard. It was so easy being with her.

"Hey, George!" Adam called as he ran past. "Want to help fly my kite?"

George watched him and the brightly colored kite bouncing in the wind against the clear blue sky full of white fluffy clouds.

"Go on," Samantha said. "I can see that you want to and I know he wants to."

"Yeah, it looks like fun, but I think I'll take off my shoes." George kicked off his sneakers and jogged out to meet Adam.

He was glad to get away. Even for a moment, because the more he got to know Samantha the harder he was falling, and that was a bad thing.

Samantha tried to read the book she'd brought, but she wasn't reading any of the words, just flipping pages as she watched George and Adam running along the beach, playing with the kite. It made her heart melt. She hadn't seen Adam as carefree and happy like this in a long time.

Usually when they came to the beach alone, he played with his kite for maybe twenty minutes and then he'd complain he was hot or tired and that he wanted to go home.

Samantha glanced at her wrist watch. Yep, they'd been here for an hour and it didn't seem like Adam showed any signs of stopping.

George was a good influence on him.

Dammit.

Why did he have to be the one man she couldn't have?

Why can't you have him?

The question caught her off guard. Why indeed? Soon she wouldn't be his teacher any more. There would be nothing like that holding her back, so what was stopping her?

Location had nothing to do with it. That was just an excuse.

Samantha sighed and set down her book.

She didn't have time for this. Falling for George wasn't part of the plan, but when did life go according to plan?

If life went according to plan she wouldn't be wrestling with her emotions about George, because she'd be with Cameron.

Only Cameron wasn't here.

He'd been gone for a long time. She'd been alone for so long.

Get a grip on yourself.

Samantha leaned back in her chair. No, she had to keep her head clear, keep things platonic with George, stay on plan. Once they parted ways she wouldn't be so tempted. She just had to get through the next month without thinking about him like this.

She could make it another four weeks.

She had strong willpower.

Who was she kidding? She had the worst willpower.

Her mother had wanted her to stay away from Cameron when they'd first met, but she hadn't listened to her mom and had gone right for the forbidden fruit.

Her mother hadn't wanted her to get married so young, she'd wanted her to focus on school and get a good job doing what she loved, but had she listened? Nope, she'd married Cameron.

And then there had been the discussion about babies.

Actually, Samantha had intended to take her mother's advice on that, but after one night with a little too much wine, she'd found herself pregnant with Adam.

Life never went according to plan and as she watched George and Adam on the beach, flying that kite like so many fathers did with their kids, Samantha found herself wondering what it would be like if she swallowed her fears to be with George.

It could be good, but it was all just a fantasy. That's what it would have to remain, because everything had been set in motion. Her job was waiting for her, she'd bought a house in Thunder Bay. A nice house with a fenced backyard where Adam could play.

There was no guarantee that if she pursued something with George it would work out. Relationships didn't have a warranty on them and Samantha had not been much of a gambler since Cameron.

Even though her heart screamed at her to give it a chance, Samantha didn't think that way.

Her head and common sense won out.

She was resolved. She and George would just be friends. There was no future for the two of them.

Which was kind of depressing.

Risk your heart, don't be chicken.

No, she knew she wouldn't, she couldn't and that was the end of it. Life wasn't fair, but who ever said it was? Life had certainly not been easy for her or fair, but she was a big girl. She wasn't going to wallow about it.

She'd move on and George would too.

"I really don't want to work tomorrow's night shift," George said.

"Me neither. I'm tired." Samantha glanced in her rearview mirror to see Adam slumped over in his seat, dead to the world.

They'd stayed in Grand Bend until the sun had set. They'd had dinner at a local burger joint and surprisingly Adam and George had gone swimming although Adam had run out screaming that it was too cold. George had splashed around for a bit before he'd admitted that, yes, the lake hadn't quite warmed up yet.

They'd walked along Grand Bend's downtown and looked through shops that catered to cottagers and beachgoers. Once the sun had begun to set they'd climbed into the minivan to head back to London.

It was now dark and Samantha would have to wake Adam up because even though she was on the ground floor there was no way she could pick up Adam any more.

"Who's watching Adam tomorrow?" George asked.

"His grandparents. They'll take him to the fireworks, like they always do."

"Right, you did tell me that."

"They'll come for him in the morning and I'll try to get some sleep during the day."

"Yeah, I'm going to keep away from coffee in the morning," George said.

"Good idea."

George shrugged. "Yeah, well, my sisters and Cheryl say coffee gets me too wired." George's easy demeanor melted away and he turned to look out the window.

"Your fiancée?" Samantha asked.

"Yeah."

The word "fiancée" caused a flash of jealousy to race through her.

Samantha cleared her throat. "What happened? I mean, why did it end?"

George glanced at her quickly. "I don't really want to talk about her."

"I shared with you." She looked at him quickly, smiling. "So what happened?"

"She left. There's really nothing more to say on the matter." Nothing more was said and even if she wanted to find out more she doubted he would open up. There was finality in his tone.

"I'm sorry to hear that."

George gave her a half-smile. "Thanks, but I really don't need sympathy."

"I understand."

She did. Sympathy was all well and good, but after a while, when you were trying to move on, the pity, the sympathetic looks and placating undertones were too much.

"Do you?" Then he groaned. "Sorry. I forgot who I was talking to for a moment."

"It's okay. I get it. It sucks." Samantha sighed.

"It can… The sympathy is hard to bear sometimes."

"I hear you and Cheryl didn't die and…" George trailed off. "Anyway, I get it. I understand."

Samantha looked at him quickly and she wondered again what had happened. Why had Cheryl left?

It's not any of your business.

And it wasn't, but she recognized the pain etched into his face. He might be trying to hide, but she recognized grief and the loss of a life partner. Even if her loss had been from death and his a break-up. Obviously it had scarred him deeply.

She'd opened up to him, but he couldn't open up to her and she couldn't help but wonder if the wound was still fresh.

"When did she leave?"

"A year ago." George shrugged. "It really doesn't matter. She's gone and I'm here."

Yeah. You are.

"So, when are you going to show me *Okla-*

homa! and some other horrible musical?" George asked, changing the topic. Something she noticed he was quite good at whenever she came too close to finding out what was buried deep inside him.

Samantha shrugged. "I don't know. When are you going to watch *Paint Your Wagon* with me?"

"We'll work it out."

Which was a polite way to say that it probably wouldn't happen, and that was for the best, but it felt like a kick in the gut.

"I know the night will drag tomorrow, but I'm hoping it's a slow night."

Samantha nodded. "Me too."

Silence descended between them. She wished it didn't have to be this way.

"I hope you had fun today," she said, breaking the silence.

"I did. Adam is a great kid."

"Thanks." Samantha cleared her throat. "You mentioned you had nephews?"

"A niece and a nephew, but they're still too

young to have any real fun with. They can barely hold their heads up."

"That's such a fun age, though. I miss that, Adam head-butting me."

"What?" George asked.

"Well, he couldn't control his head and he'd often head-butt me or push against me. I loved it when he'd do that." She sighed. "I always wanted three kids."

"You say it like you won't. You're still young. Who knows what will happen in the future?"

Her pulse began to race. "Right. It's true, but I don't think so."

"Why?"

The question caught her off guard. She'd had similar conversations with friends before, but after she said her piece they dropped it. No one had asked her why she didn't think she would have more kids.

"I'm married to my job."

She cringed inwardly at the lame excuse and she could feel George's eyes boring into her.

"You're married to your job?" he asked in disbelief.

"You don't believe me?" she asked.

"I think you're hiding behind your job."

Samantha snorted. "Oh, look who's talking."

George chuckled. "Yeah, I guess so. You were happy with Cameron, though, it's obvious. I would think you'd want that happiness again."

He was right. She would love to have that intimacy and happiness again, but she knew the pain when that was snatched away from you.

Maybe her own scars weren't as healed as she thought they were.

"Well, what about you?"

"What about me?"

"Do you want happiness again?"

George said nothing, he just turned and looked out of the window. "I don't know."

"It's hard." Samantha sighed. *So hard.*

"So, do you have your pilot's license or are you just going to work as a crew member on the plane?" George asked, breaking the tension and once again trying to change the subject.

This time Samantha was thankful for his effort.

"I do, in fact. I plan to fly the plane, not just be a crew member."

"I'm impressed. You've done amazingly well for yourself, you know that?"

"Thanks. It means a lot coming from you, especially since you piloted your own plane."

"Thanks." George turned away and she could see he was frowning. Another touchy subject.

She wanted to pull over, grab him by the shoulders and shake it out of him. Why was he throwing away such a good career? Why was he throwing away a pilot's license? It just seemed like a big waste to her.

It's not any of your business.

They didn't say anything further for the rest of the trip back to London, which made for a very tense and awkward ride. When she dropped him off at his apartment they said goodnight and exchanged pleasantries about seeing each other the following night at work.

Once she got home she roused Adam, which

was a painful process, and dragged the picnic basket inside. Everything else could stay in the car until the next morning when Adam's grandparents came.

She set down the picnic basket and rubbed her temples. Her head was beginning to pound and she felt sad.

"That was fun today, Mom," Adam said with a yawn behind her.

She turned round and Adam was in his pajamas. She put her arms around him and gave him a hug. "I'm glad you had fun today, buddy. Are you…are you okay with us moving up to Thunder Bay?"

Adam grinned. "Yeah, I am. I want to go and live up north and be near Jessie and my other cousins, and it'll be good to spend time with Nana. Grandma said she'd fly me down whenever I wanted to visit her and Gramps."

Samantha stroked Adam's head and tried to hold back the tears that were threatening to escape. "You're a pretty cool kid. I love you, buddy."

Adam rolled his eyes, but he was smiling as he tucked his head on her shoulder and squeezed. "I love you too, Mom."

He let go of her and headed down the hall to go to bed.

Samantha let out a sigh.

As much as she wanted more, a man in her life, she'd been dealt a good hand. Adam was a good kid. If this was all she was to be given, she was happy.

Adam was her life and she was going to have a good future in Thunder Bay, doing what she'd always dreamed of doing.

She didn't need anything more, even if her heart told her otherwise.

CHAPTER TEN

GEORGE WAS VERY aware that Samantha was standing close to him as they worked side by side as the days passed. They worked together seamlessly, both together and apart, just as they had done for weeks. They didn't talk more about their personal lives; she didn't ask him over. They were coworkers. It's what he had wanted from the beginning, but now he was regretting that wish.

He liked talking to Samantha, he liked working with her, and he liked Adam.

That time together at her place and Grand Bend had made him forget what Cheryl had done to him. He'd started to feel like his old self again.

Still, if Samantha didn't want it, he wasn't going to push her.

Maybe she wasn't ready to move on from her husband's death.

So he focused on studying for his final test and focused on learning as much as he could from her.

Tonight he was hoping for another quiet night shift, just like the one after Grand Bend, but usually when one wished for a quiet night, it didn't happen.

A call came in about a fire in an apartment complex in the city's east end.

George was given the wheel once again and it was a thrill to flip the sirens and race through the city streets as they headed toward the fire.

It was like he was flying again, only on the ground, but it wasn't as thrilling as being up in the air.

When they got to the accident, the scene was chaotic. Orange and red flames licked at the sky from the top of the apartment building. People were huddled under blankets and firefighters were attempting to douse the flames to stop the fire from spreading to the older Victorian homes around the apartment block.

Samantha had led them to a firefighter who'd waved them over. George pushed the gurney toward an older gentleman.

They didn't need any words as they helped the man onto the gurney.

George gave the man oxygen as Samantha assessed him.

She was so gentle with the patients, but she also didn't take any rudeness from anyone either. When a patient was being belligerent, she was on them.

Samantha was a strong, capable woman.

He was like a moth to her flame.

"Can I have some help over here?" a firefighter called out. George looked over his shoulder and then back at Samantha.

"Go. It's okay, I'll handle this patient."

George nodded and headed over to the firefighter.

"What seems to be the trouble, Captain?" George asked.

"We're bringing out a baby who is non-responsive. As soon as my man gets the child out..."

George nodded. "I'm on it."

The firefighter in question came running out of the building with the baby wrapped in a blanket. George immediately took the child from him and knelt down on the ground.

He could hear the mother screaming, crying as he assessed the ABCs on the child, but he drowned her out. All he wanted to do was focus on the baby.

George gently titled the infant's head back and opened his mouth. The airway was clear, so he placed his mouth on the baby's and breathed.

The chest rose, but there was nothing.

Come on, little guy.

With two fingers he began to compress the chest to the rhythm he remembered learning when he had first been training to become a paramedic.

When he got the number of compressions in he covered the baby's mouth and nose and breathed again. Two puffs; he watched the chest rise.

Then compressions again.

He was aware the moment Samantha knelt beside him. Out of the corner of his eye he could see the AED resting beside her. Ready if needed.

As he bent down to give some more breaths there was a cough and a thin wail.

The baby's cry sent a zing through his body. It was the best sound he'd heard in a long time.

George grinned. "Good job, buddy." He picked the child up, swaddling him in blankets.

"My baby?" the mother cried through her oxygen mask from her own gurney.

"He's breathing. He's alive. We have to get him to the children's hospital, stat." George turned and ran toward the rig, with Samantha on his heels.

He climbed in the back and Samantha handed him the oxygen mask. He cradled the baby in his arm and held the oxygen mask over his face, while Samantha made sure they were strapped in and stable.

As she hooked him, their gazes met and she was smiling at him. There was warmth in those blue eyes and it shook him to his very core. He wanted to say something, something he couldn't articulate, but she moved away. She shut the doors and then climbed into the front, flipping on the siren and calling in to the Dispatch to ready an incubator.

George glanced down at the little baby, covered in ash but alive and breathing in the oxygen. He got the rush he hadn't been feeling since his crash.

Yeah, he'd done his job, but he'd been going through the motions.

Even when he'd saved that little girl on his first day, he hadn't *felt* anything.

He'd been numb inside, but this…this affected him and he wasn't sure what to do with the feelings.

Samantha watched as George placed the baby gingerly into the incubator. The pediatric critical care staff had met them out in the emergency corridor, waiting for their charge. George kept the oxygen on the baby as the doctor and nurses hooked him up to monitors.

Samantha learned from Dispatch that the mother was being brought to the same hospital and that the baby's name was Chad.

George rattled off the vitals to the doctor as they raced down the hall toward the PCCU so they could intubate the baby and let a machine breathe for him while they surveyed the damage the smoke inhalation had done to the poor babe's lungs.

It was all much too much for Samantha to bear. The emotions George had stirred in her when she'd seen him bringing that baby around, saving the child's life…

He had been so gentle and caring as he'd cradled the infant in his strong arms, helping the baby breathe and fight for his life.

When the incubator was in the PCCU George handed over the oxygen mask, albeit a bit reluctantly, to a nurse and walked toward Samantha.

His face was covered in sweat and ashes, his

white, crisp shirt was wrinkled and smudged and she was sure she didn't look any better.

"Any word on the mother?" George asked, as he fell into step beside her.

"She's on her way here. You saved Chad's life. You were amazing tonight."

George shrugged. "All part of the job, right?"

"Right." They walked in silence side by side and she could sense a change in him. Something subtle.

"Want to grab a cup of coffee?" she asked.

"I would love some."

They wound up in the hospital coffee shop. Samantha ordered two cups of strong, black coffee and handed him one.

They headed outside to their ambulance. Not saying anything, just drinking their coffee. Once they were outside they sat in the back of the rig, much like they had that time they'd been stuck on the highway.

Only it wasn't daytime, there was no lake. Just a hospital that never slept. When Samantha looked east she could see the pink tinges, the first signs of dawn in the sky.

"You were awesome tonight," she said again.

"Thanks, but really I shouldn't be getting praise for saving a life. You were helping that man who couldn't breathe."

Samantha chuckled. "Yeah, but there's something about a handsome man saving the life of a little baby."

Then her cheeks flamed with heat as she realized what she'd just said.

"Handsome, eh?" There was a twinkle in his eyes and he winked at her before taking another pull on his coffee.

She bopped him on the arm. "Shut up." Then they laughed.

"Well, I guess you're right about the whole guy-saving-a-kid thing. I got an invitation to a big dinner thing."

Samantha cocked an eyebrow. "Big dinner thing?"

"Yeah, something about honoring local heroes."

"George! That's pretty important."

George shrugged. "It's my job to save lives. I don't think I should be honored for it."

"Are you going to turn it down, then?" she asked.

"Not if you come with me."

Samantha was dumbstruck. She should say no, but she couldn't come right out and say it. "I don't know, George."

"You're my partner. You have to come with me."

She felt a little down about that. So he was just taking his partner. This was good. She could say yes to that.

"Okay. I'll go with you. When is it?"

"Tomorrow night!" He grinned, crushing the empty coffee cup in his hand and tossing it into the garbage.

"Tomorrow, and how long have you known about it?"

"A couple of weeks."

Samantha rolled her eyes. "Men, you're all the same."

He just grinned and then got up. "So, where are we off to now?"

"Back to Dispatch. Our shift is almost over."

George nodded. "I'll drive."

Samantha tossed him the keys to the ambulance and climbed into the passenger seat.

What are you doing?

She didn't know any more. She'd kept her distance from George after their time in Grand Bend together and it was working. Or at least she thought it was, but they worked so well together. She was so at ease around him and the more she pulled away, the more she was drawn in, and now she was going to a dinner where he was going to be honored by the City of London for bravery.

Was she nuts?

Yes, completely, but she couldn't help herself and she was scared witless.

The night of the dinner, Samantha paced. It had been a long time since she'd worn a cocktail dress and had her hair done. She was fidgeting and the high heels hurt her feet.

Adam had assured her, before he'd left to go to Joyce's house, that she looked good. Really good, even for a mom.

Samantha chuckled to herself at that and checked her hair once again in the mirror. The dark green cocktail dress was something she'd bought on a whim last year and she'd never worn it. It was a halter-neck dress and hugged her body, and the hem rested above her knees. The special bra she had to wear dug into her sides, just as much as the stilettos pinched her toes.

What am I doing?

There was a buzz at the door. "George?"

"Yeah, it's me."

"Okay, come on in." Samantha hit the buzzer and began to pace.

She was going as his partner, nothing more.

She'd had to dress up and look good. They were going to a dinner thrown by the mayor. The knock at the door made her heart skip a beat. She took a deep calming breath and opened it.

When she saw him she had to check herself, because she wasn't sure that was George she was looking at. He was wearing a dark suit, which was well tailored to his muscular physique. The royal blue tie set off the dark color of his eyes and his hair. He looked dangerous—like a man who needed to be tamed, and she suddenly had the urge to be the one doing the taming.

Badly.

His gaze raked her from head to toe and her blood heated under his perusal.

"Wow," was all he said.

She blushed and reached up to play with her hair, but forgot that it was done up in a French twist.

Focus.

They were standing in her doorway, staring at each other.

"You clean up nice," she said, hoping that she

was keeping her tone at ease when her pulse was jackhammering through her body.

"Thanks. So can I escort you to the dinner?" He held out his arm.

"Of course." Samantha locked her apartment and took his outstretched arm, hoping her body wasn't shaking too much being so close to him.

You work alongside him every day. This is nothing new.

Only it was.

He led her outside and opened the car door for her. As she sat down, she saw his gaze lock onto her legs and her body flushed with a rush of heat again. He shut the door once she was seated and then got into the driver's seat.

"Seriously, you look good. Not sure if I told you that," he said.

"I think your 'Wow' got the message across."

He chuckled. "No, I don't think it did you justice."

Her heart beat just a bit faster and she suddenly didn't know what to do with her hands. He started the car and they didn't say much to each other as they drove to the plush hotel downtown.

He paid for valet parking and then escorted her inside. His arm around her was so strong against the small of her back it made her tremble with anticipation.

They were led into a reception area.

She was sure that she was making small talk, but she couldn't recall anything, because all she knew, all she could comprehend was George.

They didn't have much of a chance to talk privately as they were seated at a large table with other award recipients. George hated making small talk, but he did his best.

And when he was called up after the dinner George accepted his award, though he still didn't think he deserved it. Samantha clapped and beamed at him from the audience, giving him a thrill. After the awards had been handed out he was pulled away to talk with the mayor and some of the other bigwigs. He was failing miserably at making small talk.

He knew he should be focusing on the bigwig officials and on how he was being honored, but he couldn't take his eyes off Samantha. He'd never seen her so dressed up, except for that one wedding picture of her and Cameron on the wall of her apartment, and even then he'd barely glanced at it.

She wasn't Cameron's wife any longer. She was his widow, just like he wasn't engaged to Cheryl any longer.

Cheryl was gone.

Samantha was here and she was stunning and sexy. The green of her dress made her bronze skin glow, made her blue eyes twinkle. The dress was tight, showing off her delicious curves, and it was short, giving him a nice view of her long, long legs.

He'd only ever seen her in flats or the big clunky work boots they wore on the job. Seeing her in open-toed stilettos fired his blood and he couldn't help but picture those long legs wrapped around his waist.

He cleared his throat and pulled at the tight collar of his shirt.

It had been a long time since he'd wanted a woman.

"Cheryl, it may not be permanent. Don't leave. You don't have to leave."

Cheryl shook her head. "I want to be a pilot, George. Are you going to climb into a plane again?"

"I just crashed. I was out in the cold for almost a day. I can't honestly answer that now."

She shook her head. "Then I can't stay with you, George. It wouldn't be fair to me or you."

"What's not fair is you leaving me like this!"

"George, it wouldn't be fair if I stayed with you and I was miserable." Cheryl put on her coat. "I'm sorry. You were great, but I want more things in my life. Things you can't offer me any longer."

George shook the memory away, angry that it had intruded into his thoughts at this moment. He didn't want to think about it.

Cheryl didn't deserve his memories.

He'd think about himself and his own happiness for once. Even though he wasn't sure how he was going to achieve that.

He wasn't ready to fly again.

He wasn't ready to love again.

George searched the room for Samantha and saw her talking with the mayor's wife across the ballroom. He wished he was ready to let her in.

Samantha was only half listening to what the mayor's wife was saying. She looked up and saw George watching her intently and she smiled at him. When the music began, couples got up and started to dance.

George walked over to her and she turned her back on the women at her table, who were oblivious to her now anyway.

"You all alone tonight, darlin'?" he asked, with a wink.

She laughed and rolled her eyes. "What kind of accent were you trying there?"

"Texan?"

"It was terrible."

"Aw, come on, it wasn't that bad."

Samantha chuckled. "You sounded like Clint Eastwood. Does that make you happy?"

"It does, and you have to be nice to me. I'm a hero, you know."

"So, hero, what're you doing now?" she asked.

"Do you want to dance?" George held out his hand.

Samantha took it, hoping hers didn't shake. "I'd love to."

He led her out onto the dance floor and spun her around before pulling her into his arms. Her heart beat just a bit quicker, being so close to him.

"Thanks for saving me back there. I hate being a wallflower."

"You could never be a wallflower."

"Oh, yeah?" she said.

"I'm sure if I hadn't got to you first, another lucky soul would've asked you to dance."

"What's lurking around isn't that desirable to dance with."

George grinned. "I figured as much."

"So, if I had been approached by one of those unsavory characters lurking on the edges of the ballroom, would you have defended my honor?"

"Of course." The words were so sincere it made the butterflies in her stomach move in time with the slow music they were dancing to. She didn't hear the music. She only saw George.

Only heard his voice.

Only felt his body pressed against hers.

This was bad.

She cleared her throat. "I always have the strangest conversations with you, George Atavik."

"Is that a bad thing?" he asked.

"No, not in the least," she said softly. "I forget myself when I'm with you."

"Is that so?" The words were a husky whisper that brushed across her neck, almost making her melt.

"Did I mention how dashing you look?"

"No, you didn't." He grinned. "It's a new suit."

"Rental?"

"No, I bought it. Thought it was time."

"Well, whoever sold you the suit knows what they're doing. You're very handsome."

"I could say the same about you."

Samantha chuckled. "You think I look dashing and handsome?"

"No, not dashing Sexy. Dead sexy."

The words shocked her, and her mouth dropped open. "George—"

"No, you don't have to say anything. I'm sorry. I couldn't help myself."

"It's okay." She wanted to say she liked it, but she didn't. Her pulse was racing and she fought the urge to kiss him. She wanted to kiss him, it was so overwhelming.

He moved closer and the spicy scent of his cologne made her swoon in his arms. It was a masculine scent. She wanted to bury her face in his neck, she wanted his lips on her body, but she was too afraid to make the move.

You're chicken, Doxtator.

"Samantha," he whispered. "I should take you home. It's getting late."

He moved away from her and she nodded.

"Yeah, I think that's wise."

He led her out of the reception hall and she was glad because in his arms she came alive again and if she stayed, she might not be able to stop herself.

Leaving now was better for her heart, only it didn't feel like it.

Samantha was worried the next day that it was going to be awkward between her and George. Something had almost happened on that dance floor.

So the next night, when she showed up for their shift, she waited anxiously for him to arrive.

When he did come in, he kept his gaze focused on the floor, but instead of avoiding her he came to the table she was working at and sat down across from her, like nothing had happened between them.

George reached into his bag and pulled out a textbook, flipping it open to the middle. Samantha could see it was highlighted and there were notes scrawled everywhere.

Even though she should just get on with her reading and let him study while things were slow, she was his mentor. The least she could do was help him prepare for the exam. Her mentor had done that.

"What're you working on now?" she asked, setting her novel down.

"Nothing much," George responded, not looking up. "Just going over stuff, studying for the final test in August."

"That's really early to study for a test."

"It's the only way I'll pass. I study until it's anchored in there." He tapped the side of his head. "Also, this way I won't stress so much closer to the exam date."

"Smart move."

She wanted to say more, but the sirens went off. Samantha jumped up and ran for the dispatch desk. All the paramedics on duty were standing at the ready.

The dispatch operator took down the information and then looked up. "There was a baby born in Owen Sound. The baby needs to be air-lifted to the children's hospital. The helicopter has been dispatched."

"I'll go. I'm familiar with air transports," Samantha tossed her book in her bag and slung on her reflective coat. She was expecting George to follow her and turned, but he remained frozen to the spot. "George, are you coming?"

"No, I'll sit this one out. You won't need me for an air transfer."

George was right, he didn't have to go with her. The helicopter would have limited space, but it would be an opportunity that most para-medics in George's shoes wouldn't have passed up.

She walked over to him. "You should really come and see how it's done."

"Why? I don't plan on working in air transfer. Only in a land ambulance." He turned away, but she grabbed his arm.

"George, this is a great opportunity."

He brushed her hand away. "I've had more

than my share of time in the air. My file states that."

"You're being foolish."

George frowned, his eyes narrowing. "I'm not and you need to back off, Samantha."

She was going to say more, but she could hear the distant roar of the chopper as it came to in to land on the tarmac outside Dispatch.

"This is your last chance. Are you coming?"

"Why are you pushing me? It's none of your business."

Samantha backed off. He was right. She shouldn't care, but she did.

"I can see I'm wasting my time."

"Yeah, you are."

George didn't look back at her as he headed out to where the lockers were.

Samantha shook her head. Angry at him for being stubborn and hurt that he wouldn't give it a chance. There was no changing him.

Well, she had a job to do. One that she loved. She grabbed her kit bag and headed outside. The neon-yellow chopper landed with a slight jump on the tarmac.

Samantha kept her head down as she headed toward the spinning blades of the helicopter. The sliding door on the side opened up.

"Samantha Doxtator?" the helicopter technician shouted.

"Yes. We're headed to Owen Sound?"

The tech nodded and handed her some noise-cancelling earphones. Samantha took a seat on the bench, buckling herself in as the tech slid the door shut.

As the helicopter lifted off the ground she glanced out the window to see George standing on the tarmac, looking up at her as the helicopter rose.

Her throat constricted as she saw the look of terror and pain etched across his face, before he turned on his heel and headed back inside Dispatch.

Samantha pushed the incubator with her small charge from the hospital's helipad and into the hospital as fast as she could, but she didn't want to jar the baby. The male infant's stats were all over the place. He needed oxygen. He was too premature.

It was hard to keep her emotions in check when she glanced through the glass to see the little baby struggling for life and it had been hard taking him far away from his mother, who was still trying to recover from a crash C-section.

The tears of fear in the new mother's face had tugged at Samantha's heartstrings, but this was part of the job and as much as she'd wanted to comfort her or even shed a tear in sympathy, she hadn't.

Hold on, little guy.

She got the baby into the pediatric critical care unit where the physician on call was waiting. She helped the nurses get the baby transferred over to a hospital incubator, where they got to work intubating the baby and examining him.

When the baby was stable Samantha handed over the baby's charts and signed off.

Her job was done and it was up to the doctors now. She headed back to the helipad where the helicopter waited.

When she was inside with her headphones on, the pilot started the engine and it wasn't long before they were rising above the city. As she looked out the window she could see an explosion of brightly colored lights bursting across the dark sky.

Fireworks. Which was strange for tonight. Victoria Day was long over.

She smiled and wondered if Adam was looking at the same fireworks as she was. Could he see them as well? Then she thought of George.

The look of terror on his face as the helicopter had taken off had been unmistakable.

She was going to find out tonight what had happened to him.

She needed to know. She wanted to help him.

She cared for him and that realization of how much she did care for him, no matter how she tried to deny it, made her stomach flutter with anticipation.

It scared her.

Maybe it's time you dealt with your own ghosts.

It didn't take long before they were landing on the tarmac outside Dispatch. The main bay door was open and one of the ambulances was gone, but someone remained at Dispatch and she hoped that someone was George so they could talk.

The helicopter landed with a bump and she handed the headphones back to the tech, who opened the door. She climbed out carefully, grabbing her kit bag and ducking under the rotating blades she ran to Dispatch.

When she was a safe distance away, she turned and waved as the neon-yellow helicopter took off and headed back to the airport, where they were stationed.

With determination she headed inside. She was shaking, her stomach aflutter, when she saw that it was George who had stayed behind. He was sitting on the table, his arms on his knees and his head hanging.

When she dropped her kit bag on the counter where they were kept, his head snapped up and he looked at her.

"You're back." There was relief in his voice, but also something else she couldn't quite put her finger on.

"I am. Where's everyone else?" She peeled off the reflective jacket and hung it on a hook.

"Some drunk idiots set off some fireworks. I think you can figure out the rest."

Samantha nodded. "Are you okay?"

George stood. "Of course. Why wouldn't I be?"

"Because I saw your face when I was taking off."

George lips pressed together in a firm line, his face like thunder, and those warm dark eyes were cold, like a black hole. "I don't know what you're talking about."

"Why won't you fly? You have a pilot's license. Tell me why you won't fly."

"This discussion is over."

"I don't think so."

He turned to leave but she grabbed his arm and he spun round, pressing her against a set of lockers, his arms on either side of her head. She was frightened he was so close, but she wanted him this close to her. Maybe even closer and with nothing between them. "George, tell me. I can help you."

"Why do you want to know so badly? Can't you just let it go and accept my choice? I don't want to fly."

"I find that hard to believe."

"Why?" he demanded. "Why do you find that hard to believe?"

"You're a pilot with years of experience. You don't fly unless you love it and you don't give it up for anything unless…" Samantha trailed off as it hit her like a ton of bricks.

"You crashed."

George turned, walking quickly away from her. Though she should let him go, she couldn't, and followed him. Head first, it seemed, ignoring every rational thought running through her mind.

They were in the locker room now, alone. George had opened his locker and was getting ready to leave. Even though his shift wasn't over, he was getting ready to leave.

"You crashed the plane you were piloting?"

George paused and when he looked over his shoulder at her he didn't have to say a word to confirm that. She could see the pain etched into his face.

"It's nothing to be ashamed of, George. That would terrify anyone." She took a step closer, knowing that she was rushing headlong to her own doom. She reached out and touched him. "George, please talk to me."

"Don't touch me."

"Why?" she asked, her pulse thundering in her ears.

"Because if you do, I may not be able to stop myself from kissing you. I wanted to so badly last night and I swore I would never..." His dark eyes glittered with desire, she knew what it was because she was positive it was reflected in her eyes as well.

"What if I want you to?"

He didn't say anything. He just took a step closer, but she didn't back away. George reached out for her, pulling her close. With gentle, strong hands he cupped her face and she closed her eyes as their lips met in a kiss that seared her to her very soul.

Her body ignited and want burned deep inside her. A need she hadn't felt in so long. His kiss deepened, became more urgent and though her body screamed at her to hold on and not let go, she pushed him away, breaking the kiss.

She touched her lips, tears stinging her eyes.

"I'm sorry. I'm sorry."

She ran out of the locker room, grabbing her purse, and headed for her car. She had to get out of there, because if she'd allowed the kiss to go on, the kiss would have turned into something more. Something she wasn't sure she was ready for.

George wasn't the only one tonight with a ghost haunting him.

As she drove home, she let the tears flow.

She was too afraid of letting him in. She was so afraid of loving and losing again. She hated herself for it.

You're a coward, Samantha.

CHAPTER ELEVEN

AFTER WHAT HAD HAPPENED between them, it made for an awkward couple of weeks, but she dealt with it. The new distance between them was hard, though. She'd become so used to talking with him that she missed his company.

Samantha watched George work through a simulation on the tarmac outside Dispatch. For all those new trainees, especially the ones who would be heading up north in a week, they had set up a realistic simulation with dummies.

This simulation was of an accident at a mine.

Mines were common up north and there were often accidents with various injuries. Tomorrow's simulation would be of a forest fire.

George was triaging and moving through the simulation with expertise and the seasoned attitude of an experienced paramedic.

Samantha was proud of him.

She admired him.

It was killing her a bit knowing that after today's scenarios they would only have a week together and then they'd be heading up north, where they wouldn't see each other every day.

And then, when he had done his mandatory time in Thunder Bay, he could be assigned somewhere else.

Maybe he'll stay there, a little voice inside her head told her.

Only another little voice in her head said, *What reason does he have to stay?* She certainly hadn't been able to give him one. Why couldn't she bend and change?

There were many times she wanted to do just that, but she was too afraid.

Sometimes when they were working together, or doing a transfer of a patient, she got an inkling that he was watching her and that there was tenderness in his eyes, but the moment she saw it, it was gone.

They were friends. Nothing more. Why couldn't she just be happy with that?

I want more.

She did. She wanted so much more.

The kiss they'd shared wasn't enough.

George was finishing up on one scenario and as he tagged the dummy and got up to the next station he froze. His back was ramrod straight, his fists clenched to the side. She couldn't see his face, but she could guess what it looked like.

Every time she'd talked about flying to him, she'd seen the face he was probably making. Only there was nothing to do with flying in this simulation.

The dummy he was staring at was trapped under a piece of heavy equipment. In this case a large pipe.

Samantha set down her clipboard and made her way over to George. "George, are you okay?"

She wanted to reach out and touch him, but she couldn't and she didn't.

She couldn't because right now she was being his teacher and she didn't because that was what they'd agreed on after she'd run away from that kiss.

They'd stay friends and coworkers.

"I'm fine." The words came out through clenched teeth.

Only she didn't believe him for a second. "Do you want me to run through this scenario with you?"

George didn't respond. He didn't move.

Samantha picked up the card. "Crush injuries."

"I know."

"So what would you do?"

He looked at her and the hollow blackness of his eyes sent a shiver down her spine. She hated to see him look that way. She hated that expression on his face.

"He'll die if he doesn't get help."

Samantha frowned and looked at the dummy. The gender assigned was female. "George, you're not a doctor. You can't make that call. What you have to do is help her."

"He'll die." George looked away. "He almost died."

Sympathy washed through her. "You were trapped?"

George's head snapped back. "What?"

"You were trapped when you crashed?"

George scrubbed his hand over his face. "No. Give me the card, Samantha."

"George—"

"I said give me the card!"

Samantha handed over the card and sighed. "Are you sure you're okay?"

"I'm fine. Go back to your assessment. I'm fine." George pushed past her and knelt down beside the dummy to finish the scenario.

Samantha shook her head and headed back to where she'd left her clipboard.

There was still a wall separating them. At this moment she wasn't sure if anything could penetrate it.

Though she wished it would.

Even for a moment, because she missed him.

George stayed behind after work to clean out his locker. He had one more week in the field then he'd pack up his meager belongings from his apartment and head up to Thunder Bay, where he'd secured himself a small furnished condo. He was going to be working in Thunder Bay for some time, but even so it was just another stopping point for him.

After his time in Thunder Bay he didn't know where he'd go.

What he wanted to do was go back home, but what use would he be there if he couldn't fly?

George sat down on the bench and stared at the floor.

He wanted to talk to Samantha about what had happened during the training lesson. Only he couldn't articulate it.

Seeing that dummy trapped with severe crush injuries had just brought the whole crash back to him.

Like it was happening again. Him almost crushed, dragging his body across the snow. Fighting to live because the woman he loved was waiting for him.

And then Cheryl had walked away from him and he'd been unable to go after her.

George had worked through his own pain to build a shelter, so the driving snow wouldn't pelt his face and it would hide him from any predator. He'd built a half-igloo against the plane and waited, knowing he'd been slowly bleeding to death inside, that he'd been unable to feel his lower extremities.

He had been waiting to die.

The scenario had reopened the wound, making it raw, but it was also like a slap to the face. He couldn't do his job properly this way. He'd lose the trust of the people he was working with because they would think he was unstable and he didn't want that.

So he was afraid of flying. So what?

George cursed under his breath, stood and slammed the door of his now empty locker shut. He hated himself because he couldn't do the thing he loved.

Flying was in his blood.

He was a pilot.

So be one.

The sound of a chopper approaching caught his attention. He opened his locker and tossed his bag back in then headed out to where the ambulances were.

As he passed by the phone, it rang.

He answered it.

"Health Land and Air."

"This is chopper five-oh-five. We require a paramedic to assist us with a patient transport from Kincardine to London. Are there any available paramedics?"

"Yeah. What's your ETA?"

"Five minutes out."

"Someone will be ready."

George hung up the phone.

George swallowed the lump in his throat.

Do it.

George grabbed a jacket and slipped it on.

He took a deep breath and headed out on to the tarmac.

The bright neon-yellow helicopter was touching down. The wind whipped in his face and it reminded him of that day back in Cape Recluse when the helicopter had touched down, bringing a pregnant woman to Charlotte's clinic.

Charlotte and Quinn racing out to meet him as he'd helped the woman off the stretcher. It hadn't fazed him then and he wouldn't let it bother him now.

This was the first step.

He just had to take it.

Do it!

George shook away the ghosts of his past and took one step forward. His heart was thundering in his ears but soon after that first step followed the next until he was running toward the rotating blades, ducking under them as he climbed on board.

He was shaking but he didn't let anyone see that as he slipped the headphones over his head. The door shut and locked and the helicopter began to lift.

George closed his eyes and reached up, clutching his totem.

The bear.

It was meant to heal all.

The bear was strong.

So was he.

Within moments his heart stopped racing and he opened his eyes to glance out the window. He looked out at the city stretched out below him. The lights, the sun setting to the west, the roads and to the south where Samantha was.

He might not be able to pilot a plane yet, but this was one step closer.

He was flying without the aid of sleeping pills and a relative traveling with him. He'd work his way up to piloting and maybe when he did that, he'd finally be able to return home.

Maybe he'd finally be able to be with Samantha, but that was a long way off and there was no way Samantha would be waiting for him.

He wasn't that lucky.

The sound of knocking woke her up with a start, making her heart race. Samantha rolled over and glanced at her alarm clock.

It was three in the morning.

She got out of bed and threw on her robe, thankful that Adam was at his grandparents' house.

If there had been something wrong with Adam, Joyce would've called.

The knocking started again.

Samantha peered out through the peephole.

George?

She unlocked the door and opened it. "What're you doing here?"

"Can I come in?" he asked.

"Sure." She opened the door wider as he stepped in. She closed it. "How did you get in here?"

"Someone leaving let me in. I am wearing a paramedic uniform."

"I see that." Samantha scrubbed a hand over her face. "You got off the same time as me, like eight hours ago. Why are you still dressed in your uniform?"

"I wanted to explain what happened today."

"Today has just begun," she teased. "It's three in the morning, couldn't this have waited?"

George shook his head. "No."

"You've come to talk about the simulation. Look, George, I didn't fail you or anything—"

"Just stop talking."

Samantha crossed her arms. "Why did you come, George?"

"I almost died of crush injuries."

Samantha nodded. "Go on."

"Cheryl left me when I was injured. Said she couldn't risk being married to an invalid."

Now she understood. She knew the grief he was feeling, the wound that was so raw.

"But you're not paralyzed."

"No, but the doctors didn't know if I would walk again after I was rescued. There was swelling."

"I'm sorry. I can only imagine how hard it must be, thinking about getting in a plane again after that."

"I flew tonight."

Samantha's mouth dropped open in shock, but she snapped it shut. "What do you mean?"

"I went up in the helicopter to Kincardine."

"That's amazing."

George shook his head. "I'm not ready to take the controls yet, Samantha."

"Well, it's still a big step. You should be proud of yourself, George."

"I just wanted to explain things to you. You opened up to me. I owed it to you to finally tell you why it's been hard to let someone in again."

And before she knew what was happening she was in his arms, their lips together. He was kissing her and she wasn't fighting.

God help her, but she loved being in his arms, melting.

Though she should stop it, she couldn't. She didn't want to stop it.

She wanted to savor this moment. To take it with her when they went their separate ways.

It doesn't have to be separate ways.

"I'm sorry," he whispered breathlessly against her neck. "I shouldn't."

"No, you should." She kissed him again. "There don't have to be promises, George. Let's just have this time and see what happens."

"Samantha, if you touch me again, if you look at me a certain way…I may forget that we aren't together. I may forget that we're only supposed to be friends."

"So then forget that." She kissed him. "Give me this. Please."

He'd come to her door tonight. He'd opened up and maybe nothing would continue once they got up north, but she couldn't resist him.

The kiss deepened, his tongue melding with hers, his hands in her hair as he pressed her against her couch, his hands traveling up and down her body, chest to chest, but not skin to skin, which was what she wanted.

"Not here. My bedroom."

George groaned. "I shouldn't, but I can't resist you."

Samantha grinned as he scooped her up, holding her in his strong arms, and carried her off to bed.

If she didn't do this, she'd regret it.

And she was tired of living with regrets.

Tired of having a life of things unsaid and

undone, and though she couldn't say what she wanted to say to George, at least she could show him.

Tonight they could be connected again.

Even for a short time.

When they were in her bedroom he set her down, his gaze intent as he brushed his knuckles over her cheek. "You're trembling."

"I know." Her voice wavered. "I want you, George. So much, but I'm scared. It's been a long time since I've been with someone."

George closed the little bit of distance between them and put his arms around her. "I've wanted you too, from the first moment I saw you, I've tried to resist you. I thought…I thought I had."

He tipped her chin and kissed her and she drank him in.

She couldn't get enough of him.

"George," she whispered. Her body was trembling, but she wrapped her arms around his neck.

"If you're not ready, just tell me."

"I'm ready."

They moved to her bed. She wanted to savor this moment with him, because she wasn't sure of the future. She didn't know what else there was to come, but right now she wanted to live this.

She wanted to feel every part of him.

She wanted this memory burned into her brain.

She wanted George to take her. She had to bury the ghosts of her past.

She had to move forward with her life.

And, God help her, she wanted George to be the one to take her there, to get her past this stage.

"I hope you have protection," she said breathlessly as his kisses trailed from her mouth down her neck.

"Yes," he whispered, and then he kissed her lips again, his hands sneaking up into her hair to hold her. Then he ran his fingers through her hair. "You have beautiful hair. I've longed to do this."

She broke the kiss to unbutton and remove his

paramedic shirt, tossing it on a nearby chair. Next came the undershirt, which went over his head, exposing his chest. He still wore his bear totem around his neck and she touched it gently.

"Do you want me to take it off?" he asked, his voice hitching in his throat as she let her fingers wandering over his skin.

"No, leave it on."

She ran her hands over his bare, muscular chest, her fingers running over a jagged scar on his side.

"Was this from the crash?" she asked, lightly tracing it.

"Yes." He snatched her hand from there and brought it up to his lips, kissing her fingertips, her knuckles and then turning her hand ever so slightly to place a searing hot kiss on her wrist. The kiss made her body quiver.

She wanted nothing between them; she wanted to be joined with him. They made quick work of the rest of his clothes.

He gripped the hem of her nightgown and pulled it over her head.

She gasped at the feel of his hands trailing down to her lace panties. He tugged them down and she stepped out of them.

There was no going back now.

Her cheeks flamed red. No one had seen her naked since Cameron and she tried to shy away, but he moved her hands.

"You're beautiful." He scooped her up in his arms and carried her to the bed. Laying her down, he joined her after he'd put the condom on. He lay beside her, her leg draped over his waist as he ran his hands down over her back to her bottom.

There were so many emotions raging through her, so much she wanted to convey to him, but she was too overcome with emotion to say anything.

She just wanted to be close to George. She wanted to be a part of him.

He kissed her, gently at first, but it deepened, his tongue tangling with hers as he pressed her against the bed.

"George," she whispered. "I want you."

"I want you too."

Those dark eyes she loved so much were full of desire and her pulse thundered in her ears.

This was going to happen and she was glad George was her first since Cameron.

This felt right.

This was what she wanted.

Samantha moved and parted her legs and George moved between them, his arms on either side of her head.

"If you want me to stop—"

"No, don't stop." She ran her hands down his back. "You don't have to promise me anything. Just don't stop."

She said those words because she wasn't sure if she could promise him something.

Right now all she wanted to think about was this moment.

He moaned and kissed her on the lips, a deep sensual kiss that left her reeling. She could feel his erection pressing against her. He was taking it slowly, but she wanted him to claim her. She arched her back, grabbed his butt and pulled him closer.

"Oh, God," he cried out as he thrust forward and filled her. "Oh, God."

She began to rock her hips, encouraging him as he slowly started to move.

"Faster," she begged.

"No, I want to take my time with you. I want to remember this moment of being buried inside you."

She clutched his back, holding onto him, like if she let him go it would all just be a dream, like it really hadn't happened, and she didn't want that.

His words made her swoon—literally swoon—and she melted further.

"You feel so good," he whispered against her neck as he kissed her there, moving with her. "So good."

She wanted to tell him everything she was feeling, but she couldn't get the words out. So she just felt.

She tasted his skin, ran her fingers through his

hair, their bodies pressed together. They moved as one. His hands on her were so strong and re-assuring Samantha wanted to cry, because she'd never thought that she would get to feel this way again, that she would allow another man into her bed like this.

It didn't feel wrong at all. It felt so right. It scared her and thrilled her at the same time.

"So beautiful," he murmured in her ear, as his tempo increased. "So damn beautiful."

"George," she murmured, but he silenced her words with another kiss. His hands then moved to her hips, shaping her movements, keeping them tightly joined together. He was in control, guiding her body into release.

The sweet release she craved so desperately, which she'd been denied for so long.

It didn't take long before she came, arching her back and crying out, clutching the pillows. George soon followed, his thrusts becoming shallower, faster until he stilled and climaxed.

She felt boneless as he moved to the side, bringing her with him, not letting her go. Their hearts raced in time. She lay across his chest, listening to the familiar sound of it.

"I won't stay. I know you don't want me to stay. I know this was a one-time thing."

Samantha reached out and caressed his cheek. "No, stay."

"I shouldn't."

"Stay for a bit, then. I just want you to hold me."

"Okay."

She laid her head against his chest, listening to the steady rhythm of his heart. His strong arms wrapped around her, holding her tight.

Don't let me go.

Samantha closed her eyes and drifted off to sleep.

CHAPTER TWELVE

SAMANTHA WOKE UP after a short nap and when she did she realized George was gone. There was no note, no words. Nothing. And though the doubts plagued her mind, she realized he'd left because Adam would be coming home soon. Joyce was dropping him off at eight-thirty a.m., before school started.

She got up anyway and headed to the kitchen. It was almost seven. She might as well start her day. She prepared a pot of coffee and as she stretched a memory of George's lips on her skin hit her.

Gooseflesh brushed across the spot and she smiled.

What had happened had been magical and she'd remember it always. She hadn't asked for promises when they'd made love. She hadn't needed any.

She wasn't sure if she wanted any, she didn't know what she wanted.

While the coffee was brewing she had a shower and was ready when Adam came in the door.

"Hey, Mom!" Adam paused and looked her up and down. "Whoa. You look scary!"

"Thanks, buddy. I appreciate that." She opened the fridge and pulled out his lunch. "Here you go."

"It's okay. Grandma made me a special one."

Samantha sighed and stuck the lunch back in the fridge. "I'm going to start packing today so don't be all freaked out when most of your stuff is packed up. The movers are coming in a couple of days to move us up to Thunder Bay."

"Mom, did you forget you volunteered to help out with my class trip today?"

Dammit. She had forgotten.

"Right. Of course."

"It's okay if you're tired, Mom. You don't have to."

Samantha grabbed him and hugged him. "I

want to, you knucklehead. Come on, let's go to school, then."

Adam grinned and picked up his backpack. Samantha grabbed her purse and followed him out. She wouldn't let Adam down.

Samantha stifled numerous yawns as she wandered through the art gallery. The kids were loud and she just wanted to bury her head under the pillow and sleep for a hundred years.

She wasn't really needed. There were a lot more parents on the trip than she'd thought there would be, but she didn't go back on her word.

She kept her promises.

So she dragged herself through the gallery, trailing after the group she was assigned to, which included Adam and a couple of his friends. And, of course, she had to have the most boisterous group.

When they got to a hands-on section of the gallery, where the tour guide was leading the kids in some art production, she was finally able to sit down. She leaned back against the wall and tried to keep her eyes from closing.

"You look tired, Ms. Doxtator."

Samantha glanced up to see another mother looking at her with sympathy. Samantha managed a half-smile for her. "I've been working some long shifts. Had a bit of a sleepless night. I think my schedule is off."

Only that wasn't what had caused her exhaustion.

And as she thought about it, snippets played over in her mind, making her body react with desire and need. Coupled with fear.

Give it a chance. Only she wasn't sure she could. It had been too long.

"Long shifts and preparing to move? I have to say, my daughter's going to miss having Adam in her class when you go. Where are you moving to?"

"Thunder Bay. I've been trying to get everything packed and organized. I leave at the end of the week, but Adam is staying with his grandparents to finish out the year."

"Geez, then you are really tired, eh? Why don't you go grab yourself a cup of coffee? I can watch this brood."

I need more than a cup of coffee. I need a shot of something in it.

Maybe a few shots of liquor wouldn't go amiss.

"Thanks, I think I'll do that."

"You go on. They'll be occupied here for a while."

Samantha nodded and headed away from the group they were responsible for. She was so preoccupied with George. She'd promised herself that she wouldn't get involved with him, that she wouldn't pursue anything, but when it came to him she was so very, very weak.

She didn't know what she was going to do about it.

The look on George's face when she'd been flying away in that helicopter had sent chills down her spine.

Even though he had made an incredible breakthrough with the flight to Kincardine, she knew his crash still haunted him. She didn't want him to worry and stress every time she went up in a plane, especially if he had already lost someone because of a crash.

Samantha knew what it was like to lose someone and she didn't want George to feel any more pain. He didn't deserve that.

Not after what had happened to him. That woman who'd left him because he might have been left paralyzed didn't deserve George. He was better off without her. Even though she didn't know Cheryl, she knew what had been done to George had scarred him.

It was a horrible thing to do to someone.

He was still struggling to heal.

So being with him wasn't fair to him, neither was giving up the life she'd worked so hard for. Though she had no doubt that being with him would be wonderful and maybe even magical, the timing was all off. Maybe if they'd met in a couple of years' time…

This wasn't their time.

She stopped when she realized she was walking in the wrong direction. The coffee shop and cafeteria were the other way. She'd wandered into another part of the art gallery, one that boasted a Canadian art exhibit.

As Samantha looked around she realized was surrounded by Inuit art and in particular one painting stood out amongst the rest because it was so large and vividly colored. The orange and blues popped out and the black that outlined it all was so vibrant.

The painting was of a bear.

When she approached it she realized she was staring at an Anernerk Kamut painting. George's grandmother.

She'd seen work by Anernerk Kamut, but not this big and not this close.

The title was written in Inuktitut, but then under it was the English translation, which simply said "George".

Samantha smiled.

She'd done the painting for her grandson. For his totem.

A bear was a sign of healing.

Or at least that was the teachings.

Samantha wasn't so sure about that.

She turned on her heel and headed off to find coffee, because she wasn't too sure she believed in signs.

George got up and started to pack for his move to Thunder Bay. He was tired from nights of tossing and turning, compounded by what had occurred between him and Samantha only hours ago.

Samantha.

He'd told her what had happened with Cheryl. Not even his sisters knew the real reason why Cheryl had left. He'd just said it hadn't worked out, because he was so ashamed about what had happened.

Yet Samantha had got through to him. He could still taste her on his lips, hear her soft sighs of delight and the way that pink had risen to her cheeks when he'd run his hands over her body.

She blushed so easily. He loved that about her. It suited her.

On the outside she tried to be this hard-as-nails woman and she probably needed to be, given her situation, but underneath it all she was soft and feminine.

Still, there was a part of her hidden away from him.

She was afraid of moving on. He understood that all too well.

He wished he could help her heal, but if he tried then he'd have to let her through the barriers he'd erected for himself. That scared him.

When he'd made love to her, he'd thought that night might purge her from his system. That it might sate the desire he had for her. He had been wrong. It hadn't.

I'll never get enough. And that realization stunned him. Could Samantha possibly feel the same about him?

Even when he'd taken her in his arms, she'd asked for nothing. All she'd wanted had been that moment. It had taken every ounce of strength to walk away from her when she'd been wrapped up in his arms. He'd wanted to stay with her, he hadn't wanted to walk away, but he'd known that Adam would be coming home soon and it wouldn't have been right for the kid to see him in his mother's bed.

Well, not yet anyway.

Not ever. Remember, career is your focus. Not love.

With a groan he glanced at the clock. It was four in the afternoon. He pulled a couple more shirts out of the dresser and tossed them into the open suitcase.

George rubbed his tired eyes. He couldn't think straight.

When he closed his eyes, all he saw was Samantha. All he could feel was her and just thinking about her made him want her again.

He'd been a fool to have thought that once would be enough.

He should never have gone to her apartment. He was a weak man when it came to her.

Maybe a cold shower would help relax him or at least soothe the heat in his blood.

"You're a stubborn ox, George Atavik."

George shook his grandmother's voice from his head. This was not what he needed now. Right now he needed to focus on getting his life packed up and head to Thunder Bay where he'd work in an ambulance with a new partner.

Though a new partner was the last thing he wanted.

I want Samantha.

With a sigh he got up from his futon and was shuffling toward the bathroom when there was a knock on his door. Groaning, he went to it and looked through the peep-hole, his heart skipping a beat when he saw it was Samantha.

"Samantha, what're you doing here?" George asked as he opened the door.

"I don't know. Can I come in?"

George opened the door wider and stood to the side, letting her into his modest bachelor pad. When she was inside he shut the door.

"This is sparse," she teased, a twinkle in her eyes.

"Well, it's a short-term furnished rental since I'm going to be heading to Thunder Bay in a couple of days, and then from then on, who knows?"

The smile disappeared and she nodded. "I thought you wanted to stay in Thunder Bay."

George shrugged. "I don't know if I'll stay there."

Liar.

"Shouldn't you be at home with Adam?" he asked, moving past her into the kitchen. He knew logically they needed to talk about what had happened between them early this morning, but he didn't really want to admit to the reality of it.

"I dropped him off with my in-laws after school."

"They've been taking him a lot, haven't they?" George asked.

"They're trying to spend as much time as they can with him before we move up north. Besides, it helps me pack and get ready for the movers without him underfoot."

George nodded and gripped the kitchenette's counter, like he depended on it for dear life, because he was going to keep his emotions in check. He was going to resist the urge to pick her up and carry her over to his futon and show her exactly how he felt.

"Would you like something to drink?" he asked instead.

"Sure. What do you have?"

"Good question." George opened the fridge, which was a little sparse. "I have water and some questionable milk."

Samantha chuckled. "Some water will be fine."

George pulled a bottle of water out of the fridge and brought it to her. Samantha took a seat on the one chair he had in his apartment. He sat down on the edge of the futon.

"I went on a trip with Adam's class today."

"Oh, yeah?"

"We went to a London art gallery and I stumbled across a very large painting your grandmother did."

Now he was interested. "Really? Which piece?"

"It was a bear."

George's heart warmed and he grinned. "Was it titled *George*?"

"How did you know?"

"You wouldn't be here if it wasn't that painting."

Her mouth opened and then she blushed. "Well, that was one of the reasons."

"Oh, yes?" he replied, praying that his voice didn't convey any hope.

"I wanted to talk about what happened between us."

"Yeah," he sighed. "I wanted to talk to you about that too."

"You did?"

Could it be that she felt something too? Was she hoping for some fight from him? George got up and knelt in front of her, though being so close to her was excruciating.

Fight for her.

"I understand how you feel, Samantha. How you can't…" He trailed off because he didn't want to think about the inevitable.

"I want you know how much that meant to me, the one time we shared. I wanted it, don't think that I didn't." She touched his cheek.

"It meant a lot to me too." He kissed her on the lips, but only lightly. It was so hard to pull away when he did, but if he didn't he would never be able to. "I know you don't want anything serious right now."

"I just can't see a future." She hesitated as if she was going to say something further, but she snapped her mouth shut. "I want us to stay friends, George. You get along so well with Adam and he adores you."

George nodded. "He's a good kid."

He wanted to ask her how she felt about him, but he didn't. If he poked at that dyke, it might burst.

Fight for her.

Only he couldn't. It was too hard.

Instead, they said nothing and he got the feeling she was waiting for him to say more. With a sigh Samantha stood. She set down the unopened and untouched bottle of water. George stood with her.

He was fighting the urge to pull her in his arms, to beg her to stay with him and let him make love to her, but he fought it. He fought it hard.

Still she stood there. Maybe she was fighting with the same inner demons he was.

Tell me why.

He wanted her to open up to him. He wanted her to tell him why there was no future for them. What was holding her back?

Finally she smiled, but it was forced. He could tell. Despite her defenses, he could read her.

"I'll see you at work tonight." She moved past him and headed to the door.

"Yeah, I'll see you tonight."

Samantha gave him one last look and headed out, leaving him alone in his sparse apartment. George cursed under his breath. He was such a coward.

He turned and headed over to the small balcony he had. He didn't really like the balcony, because it was small, rickety-looking, but he stood there, letting the wind blow over him as he looked across the city.

London was a big place with a large population, but here he felt alone, even surrounded by people.

When he'd started hanging out with Samantha and working with her, the loneliness hadn't affected him as much.

He'd felt connected somehow.

George looked up into the sky and saw the white contrail of a plane across the blue and a pang of longing hit him like he hadn't felt since the crash.

He missed being in the sky. He missed the feeling of a plane's controls in his hands, of being above the clouds.

George closed his eyes and for a moment it was like he was back in that little Cessna's cockpit. He was flying over the snow-capped mountains and ice-jammed waters around Baffin Island.

The ice air strip into Cape Recluse glittering

in the bright sun, for only a few hours a day, but those few hours were wonderful.

Beside him was Ambrose, or if there was a patient being transported, he'd be in the back, dealing with them.

At home he was greeted by his sisters, his parents and his friends. And then Cheryl came along.

They were partners, best friends and then lovers.

He didn't think life could get any better. They were so happy. Plans were being made. He was going to finally have a family of his own, like Charlotte and Mentlana had.

"May day, may day."

George's fists clenched on the metal railing and it felt like the world was falling out from under his feet.

It was like he was back in that cockpit, the instruments failing, the lights flashing and the only sound the rush of the plane falling and Ambrose yelling, *"Brace for impact!"*

George couldn't even really remember the

impact. He remembered waking up and being cold. He had been out of the cockpit, lying in the snow. He had been hurt, but had been able to move.

What he'd been unable to figure out had been why he'd been lying in the snow. How had he got there? Then it had all came rushing back to him and made his head hurt.

Then he'd realized he was alone.

He'd got up as fast as he could, but he couldn't feel his legs. They'd refused to work. So he'd used his arms, his lungs burning as he'd sucked in bitterly cold air, and crawled towards the remnants of the plane to seek shelter.

The roaring sound of the wind and thoughts of death had haunted him. As he'd huddled under the snow, he'd known there was no way any one could find him. He was going to die. He'd braced himself for the thought that the last thing he would hear was the howling of the snow-storm and the numbing cold burning his flesh.

Death had stalked him on that frozen tundra, but it had lost.

Just when he'd been about to give up, the rescue crew had found him and got him to Iqaluit.

George opened his eyes and looked up at the sky again. The white contrail was dissipating in the atmosphere.

He wondered where the plane was going, just like he was wondering the same about himself.

He wondered if he could ever step into a plane's cockpit again and was the promise of possibly having a future with Samantha enough to push him to try. How could he ask her to forget her fears if he couldn't overcome his own?

He hated what Cheryl had done to him, but he couldn't blame her for his current problems. This wasn't about her, it was about him.

He hated it that Samantha didn't want them to be a couple, that she couldn't see a future for them.

He hated it that he didn't fight for her.

He hated letting her go.

CHAPTER THIRTEEN

SAMANTHA SAW GEORGE from across the crowded room and her heart skipped a beat, her knees knocked together.

It had been three weeks since she'd gone to his apartment. Three weeks since she'd walked away.

They'd worked together that one last night, but they hadn't had any calls. It had been a quiet, long night. He'd studied for his final test and she'd done paperwork.

And then he was gone, his locker cleaned out before she'd even had a chance to say anything to him. To tell him that her letting him go was for the best, because she didn't want him to ever feel the pain she'd felt the day Cameron had died.

It was bad enough she thought about Adam

having to go through it, she didn't want to drag George into it.

When she'd opened his cleaned-out locker she'd found a large brown envelope. She'd opened it and in there had been a DVD copy of *Paint Your Wagon* with a note that said he was sorry they hadn't got to watch it together.

It had nearly broken her heart in half.

She'd been a fool.

His absence had left her feeling empty. It had left a hole in her heart, similar to the one Cameron had left, but different.

She loved George.

She'd tried not to, but she did. She'd fallen in love with him.

The drive up to Thunder Bay had been lonely, but on her arrival she'd been kept busy by settling into her house. Her sisters had filled the empty void, but, still, even as she'd got her life back in order, when she was alone at night in her bed she thought about George and what he was doing.

She went to work at the airfield and got assigned a crew.

They worked well together, but often when she was doing busy work she looked up, expecting to see George there. Only he wasn't. Her new crew didn't know what she needed or wanted when they were working together, not the way George had.

Samantha knew he was working in a dispatch office in downtown Thunder Bay.

Every time she heard the distant wail of a siren she wondered if he was there and she was mad at herself for being so preoccupied by him.

She understood him. They'd been through the same pain, even though their circumstances had been different. They'd both loved and lost. That was a hard thing to overcome.

And now here he was, in front of her once again. As if sensing that she was staring at him, George glanced up and looked at her. Samantha held her breath, hoping that he wouldn't look away quickly or just brush her off.

George grinned, his dark eyes twinkling as

he made his way through the crowd toward her, and she let out a sigh of relief. She didn't even realize she'd been holding her breath.

"Howdy, stranger!" George was grinning in that friendly, affable way he always did, which put her at ease, but it was still awkward when they were standing face to face. She didn't know if she should reach out and hug him or what.

"Hey, how have things been going?" she asked, trying to make small talk.

"Good, very busy. How about you?"

"Not as busy as working in an ambulance, I'm sure, but I have a good crew. How are yours?"

George smiled. "Good enough. Not as good as you, though."

"I was thinking something similar about my crew. We worked well together."

"Has Adam come up yet?" he asked.

"No, he and Joyce fly in in a couple of days."

"I bet you'll be glad to see him."

"Yeah, it will be great to have him back. I wanted him to finish out the school year, though."

She wanted to ask where he was living. She wanted to ask him if she could see him. There were many things she wanted to ask him, only she couldn't, and she didn't offer up any information either.

"Why do you think they've called us all here?" George asked.

Samantha shrugged. "I have no idea. Look, George, I wanted—"

"Can everyone take their seats?" the chief paramedic said from the podium.

Samantha groaned inwardly. "Shall we sit?"

"Might as well."

They took seats near the back. She sat with her back ramrod straight and she was very aware of how close they were and how awkward it was.

What the heck was wrong with her? This didn't have to be this way. She could tell him what she wanted. She could just reach out and take him.

She deserved happiness.

She deserved another chance. He deserved another chance.

Instead, she said nothing as the director of Health Air and Land Services stood at the podium.

"Thank you all for being here. I've called you here today because there's currently a large forest fire spreading north of Lake Nipigon. Bombers are on the move and firefighters are combating the fire the best they can, but there are several remote communities located in the fire zone."

A screen was lowered and a map was projected, showing several villages and the widespread fire.

"Hell," George whispered under his breath.

"Never seen a forest fire before?" she asked.

"There are hardly any trees in Nunavut. This is crazy."

"It is."

"We need air crews to go in and land in these communities to evacuate people. Most of these small communities are under fifty people and our aircraft can accommodate them. Large communities like Gull Bay will be evacuated by the army. Land crews will meet the planes as they land and take any injured to local hospitals. Emergency rooms are on standby for traumas. See your team leaders, get your assignments and, remember, stay safe out there."

The crowd broke up and people moved into action.

"Samantha," George whispered.

"Yes?" She waited for something. Some acknowledgement.

George rubbed the back of his neck and she waited for the words. Like a fool, she waited for him to make the first move.

"Stay safe," he said.

She wanted to tell him to come with her, but she didn't. "You too."

George gave her a quick kiss on the cheek and then turned away. She watched him as he left the meeting room.

Samantha berated herself again for taking the coward's way out.

You don't always get a second chance.

She'd had more than that, but she couldn't

bring herself to say the words and she didn't have time to think about it now.

Right now she had a job to do.

George's stomach was clenched in a series of knots that felt like they were being pulled in different directions.

As he stepped outside, even though they were kilometers away from the fire, he could smell it. There was a haze in the air. He looked toward the north and saw smoke rising in the distance.

He'd seen forest fires on television, read about them in the paper, but it was a very different experience to be close to ground zero, as it were.

As he tore his gaze from the rising smoke he caught sight of Samantha and her crew climbing into the truck that would drive them to their plane.

His stomach clenched again at the thought of her in harm's way.

Up in the sky, where the smoke obscured everything.

He missed her.

That night he'd gone to her apartment he'd wanted to tell her how he felt about her, to tell her he'd try to do anything, even face his fear, to be with her.

Only nothing had come out. He'd been distracted by her plea to make love to her. Just that simple request and he'd been a lost man.

He supposed he could have said something when she'd come to his apartment, just before they'd left for Thunder Bay, but then she'd said she saw no future for them, and it had seemed wrong to try and convince her otherwise.

When he'd arrived in Thunder Bay he'd wanted to look for her. Shout through the streets to find her, but his job was so busy and, besides, Thunder Bay was a big place.

Being busy at work gave him less time to think about Samantha, but just less.

She was always there.

Like a ghost.

Haunting him. Not only did the ghosts of his past torment him but now the living were too.

Only he could fix the later, if he would just take the chance.

He needed something to take his mind off the fact that Samantha was about to go up in a plane, landing in a zone that was being evacuated.

"Come on, Atavik!" his new partner shouted.

"I'm coming." George glanced back at Samantha one more time as her truck disappeared around the corner, and he made a vow to himself that the moment her plane landed and this was all over, things were going to change, because sometimes you just didn't get second chances.

CHAPTER FOURTEEN

THE SMOKE WAS thick in the air, but Samantha was getting used to flying through it. When she'd landed in her first small village to evacuate she'd watched in awe as large water bombers coming from Lake Nipigon had flown overhead to drop their load on the fires.

They all had their job to do.

When she landed in Thunder Bay to drop off the evacuees, she saw all the rigs lined up, waiting for those who needed to go to the hospital.

The ambulance waiting for her airplane wasn't George's.

She was a bit disappointed, but she was sure he was busy helping those who needed it. Like she was.

Once the first round of evacuees were off the plane and taken care of Samantha and her crew headed back on board, making sure everything had been restocked by the crew on the airfield.

Her co-pilot gave the all-clear and they took off with permission from the tower. This time the village they were heading to was a little further north, in the midst of the fire.

The smoke was thicker.

It was harder to see, but the instruments told her they were headed in the right direction and every now and then the smoke cleared enough to get a glimpse of the sky and the ground below.

"The fire is doing a lot of damage. I haven't seen one this big in a while," her co-pilot, Jimmy, remarked.

"No?"

He smiled at her. "We'll get everyone out. Don't worry. We're trained for this."

Samantha nodded.

She remembered going through her scenarios when she'd been starting out. She'd done the extra scenarios for the air and a mass evacuation from a forest fire had been one of them.

"This settlement has only ten people?" Samantha asked as she adjusted her instruments. "That seems quite small."

Jimmy shrugged. "It was an old trading post, back in the days of fur trappers, but now it's a logging camp, but a small one. They have a doctor and some loggers."

"It seems odd that they don't have a plane when they're this isolated," Samantha mused.

"Why do they need a plane when they have us?"

"Good point."

Then she couldn't help but think about the job George used to do. He'd told her about his sister Charlotte and how they'd worked together. Both doctor and paramedic had known how to fly. There hadn't been regular air transit for them up there.

The people of Cape Recluse had paid for the service and George had run it.

He should be leading his own team.

He should be in the sky. He would do amazing things on the air crew, because he was an amazing man.

Samantha smiled. As soon as this was all over she was going to find him and tell him. She was going to tell him she wanted to be with him.

She wasn't going to let him get away.

Sure, she was putting her heart at risk. Something could happen to George, but something could happen to her too.

She couldn't live her life in fear like this. What was that teaching her son?

She didn't want Adam to grow up and not take risks. She wanted Adam to live.

I deserve to live too.

Cameron had wanted her to move on. She knew that, because in one last moment of lucidity before the brain tumor had taken him he'd told her to find love again. Not to linger with ghosts. He'd wanted her to be happy.

At the time she hadn't been able to imagine that, but through the years she'd yearned for it again.

And the only person she could picture herself moving on with was George.

Even if he didn't want to fly again, she didn't care. They'd figure it out.

Ever since Cameron had died she'd focused on what needed to be done to ensure the best kind of life for her and Adam.

She spent so many years planning, saving and making sure things happened according to schedule.

Plans were stable. Planning had made her forget her loneliness.

It was something she could rely on, when really all she needed was *someone* she could rely on, and George was that man.

Risks were scary. Risks could get you hurt or killed, but life was all about risks.

She'd taken a chance on Cameron when she'd first met him. She'd taken a chance that night when she and Cameron had conceived Adam.

Life was messy.

It was time to get her hands dirty again.

Samantha smiled to herself.

Even if George didn't reciprocate her feelings when she told him, at least she'd know. At least she could move on and she wouldn't spend the rest of her life wondering what if.

"Coming in to the logging camp," Jimmy said.

"Roger that." Samantha peered down and through the smoke she could see the landing strip clear cut in the forest. About three kilometers from the airstrip she could see the fire's smoke, dark and thick, and through the brush she could see some flames, but they weren't high. They were low and fast-spreading.

Just then the plane jolted.

"Holy moly, that wasn't turbulence!" Jimmy shouted.

Samantha rushed to steady the plane, but the engine shuddered again, the instruments lit up and an alarm went off. The engine was failing.

"Mayday. Mayday. Tigawki Logging Camp. This is Medic Air 150. We have engine failure. I repeat, engine failure. We are making a forced landing on your airstrip. Clear the area. I repeat, clear the area. One thousand feet, descending, heading one eighty."

"Roger that, Medic Air 150."

Samantha gripped the controls, preparing herself for an emergency landing. She'd gone through simulations, but simulations were nothing compared to the real thing.

"Brace for impact!" Jimmy called out over his shoulder.

The ground was coming up faster than she wanted. There was a grinding sound as Jimmy was able to bring the landing gear down manually.

Samantha said a prayer.

She prayed that God wouldn't let her die. Adam still needed his mother.

She prayed her crew would make it and as the plane shuddered and she heard metal scraping, she thought about George and the chances she hadn't taken.

"Bob has smoke inhalation. His crew is grounded," George's partner Finn said, wiping his brow. There was soot on his face.

George nodded and coughed to clear his throat. "His last evacuation got a little too close?"

Finn nodded. "We're down one plane, but that's okay. We're going to get everyone in the affected area out."

George nodded. "Good."

He squinted and then he heard the roar as a water bomber flew overhead. The fire was getting a little closer to Thunder Bay, so the bombers were starting to get water from Lake Superior to battle the encroaching flames.

The smoke was thicker and the airfield was chaotic as an army plane coming from one of the larger communities landed.

George headed into Dispatch.

The moment he walked through the door he knew something was wrong. He could feel it deep in his bones.

The chief was shaking his head and cursing.

"Chief, what's wrong?" George asked with dread, because he knew. He just knew. A plane had gone down and he hoped it wasn't Samantha's.

Oh, God. Don't let it be her.

"Medic Air 150 went down on the approach

to Tigawki Logging Camp. All my planes are out, except for Bob's. The fire is really close to the camp."

George felt his world crumble.

He knew Samantha's call number.

"Survivors?"

The chief shook his head. "We don't know. The fire has cut communications with the logging camp. We know the plane went down as it was landing. We'll try to get help to them as soon as we can, but the military plane is too large to land there and they're still unloading evacuees."

George's soul screamed. He wanted to drop to his knees and curse, but she could be still alive. No, she *was* still alive. He'd know if she'd died.

Samantha was smart. She was still alive.

"Bob's plane is back," George said.

"Bob has smoke inhalation and we don't have another pilot."

Courage.

"Yeah, you do. Me."

The chief eyes widened. "You, you're a pilot?"

"Yes, sir. You can check my files, but this will

help." He pulled out his wallet and showed him his pilot's license. "Let me take Bob's plane and crew to Tigawki. I'll bring them all back."

The chief nodded. "Well, get it, Atavik. We'll clear you for take-off as soon as you're ready." The chief laid in a rush call to restock Bob's plane while George rounded up Bob's co-pilot and crew.

All of them were willing to go.

He climbed on board the plane. The rest of the crew were furiously getting ready to take off. George's pulse was thundering in his ears as he headed to the pilot's seat.

I can do this.

With a deep breath he sat down and went over the controls. He remembered it all and as he gripped the controls his hands remembered what to do.

I can do this.

It was like riding a bike.

"You can do this. You can save her. She won't die."

The words in his head came in his grandmother's voice. Even in the afterlife she was doling out words of wisdom to him. George nodded in response. Yeah, he could do this.

His co-pilot took her seat. "You ready to go, George?"

George glanced over at Christine. "Are we ready?"

She nodded. "Just waiting for clearance."

George flicked on the controls and the plane started. The whirring of the engine was all too familiar.

"Tower, this is Medic Air 60, waiting for clearance."

"Medic Air 60, this is Tower, you're clear for take-off on runway three."

"Roger that." George taxied out of the hangar and headed toward the runway. The engine roared in his ear as he took the plane onto the tarmac and gained speed. When they were at the correct velocity he pulled back on the controls and the plane lifted into the air. The green forest disappeared from his view, to be met by the hazy, smoke-filled sky.

There was a whir as the wheels retracted under the plane.

George brought the aircraft to a safe altitude and leveled off. Christine was busy with her work and George guided the plane onto the correct heading to Tigawki Logging Camp.

"Last report we had was that the plane crashed into the woods at the end of the runway. We should have room to land."

George nodded and kept his focus on the sky.

He didn't want to think of Samantha hurt or lost in the woods, like he'd been lost in the snow at the mercy of the elements.

He didn't want to think of her body broken under a piece of the plane.

She's okay.

She had to be okay.

It didn't take long before they neared their destination, but for George it felt like an eternity. The smoke was thick, but George could see water bombers not too far off, scooping up water from a nearby lake and dropping it on the forest below.

"Tigawki Logging Camp, this is Medic Air 60 requesting permission to land." George waited for an answer, hoping that they could get through, that those lines hadn't been severed.

"Medic Air 60, this is Tigawki Logging Camp. Permission to land granted. You're a sight for sore eyes. We have a lot of wounded paramedics here, our doctor has triaged them, but some are in a bad way."

God, no.

George's heart stuttered. "Roger that."

"Preparing to land," Christine said.

There was a whir as the landing gear came down. George began to land the plane.

Christine cursed out loud as they caught sight of the smoking wreckage of Medic Air 150 scattered at the edge of the forest.

Focus.

George landed the plane and brought it to a stop at the end of the airstrip.

Once it was safe, they got busy, grabbing kits as they jumped off the plane. The logging camp's physician came running toward the plane with someone strapped to a stretcher.

George felt his throat constrict.

Two paramedics from the plane George just landed helped load it.

George walked out among the wreckage. His mind raced with a thousand thoughts and he had a hard time breathing through the smoke.

It was like they were in the middle of a war zone. Like a bomb had gone off, the forest around the airstrip had been so altered. Large trees felled, random fires and the clear-cut airstrip torn up as the plane had broken apart into three smoking sections.

There was a roar of thunder above them as a water bomber streaked through the air.

"Get the evacuees on board!" George shouted.

He dropped to the side of another paramedic, Samantha's co-pilot Jimmy, who was lying on a stretcher, injured but still conscious. "What happened?"

Jimmy winced. "Engine failure."

"Is everyone…? Did anyone…?" He couldn't finish the words.

"Everyone's alive. Just Mike got the brunt."

A couple of loggers came over and George directed them to take Jimmy to the plane while he assisted the other injured paramedics. All the while he was searching for Samantha in the chaos. He had to find her.

He had to take her to safety and then never let her go.

Please, God. Let me find her.

He hoped his silent prayer wasn't falling on deaf ears.

George made his way through the wreckage. His eyes scanned the scene constantly, searching for her as he dodged pieces of debris and broken trees. He was worried she was lost in the carnage, like he had almost been.

I survived. I'm here and Samantha is out there and she's alive.

George wouldn't accept anything less.

His pulsed hammered in his ears like thunder, drowning out the din and confusion from the crash site.

Please.

George took a deep breath a moved toward the huge piece of fuselage that was smoldering further away. As he approached the edge of the forest, he saw something through the smoke. Someone on the ground, with a paramedic kneeling beside them.

No. Oh, God.

As he got closer the kneeling figure stood up and through the haze of the smoke he saw it was Samantha and he relaxed.

She wasn't trapped under the fuselage. She was up and walking, and as he watched her he could see she was triaging people. She was fine. She was alive.

George let out a silent prayer of thanks as he approached her. As she did her job he saw her head was bandaged and some blood was coming through the gauze.

She was rummaging through a first-aid kit when he caught up to her.

"Need a hand?"

Samantha spun around. Her eyes widened when she saw him and he winked at her. "George? Is that you or am I hallucinating?"

"No hallucination. I'm the real thing."

She let out a sigh of relief and touched her bandaged head. "Thank God. For a second there I was worried that I might have a concussion."

He stepped forward and touched her head. "Can I look?"

"Sure."

Gingerly he unwrapped the bandages and she winced as he examined the gash in her forehead. "Might need some skin glue, but I think we'll get you to the hospital and they'll do an X-ray anyway to rule out a concussion."

"Are you sure I'm not hallucinating?" She chuckled and sucked in a deep breath as he wrapped up her wound.

"No, you're really not."

Then her brow furrowed in confusion. "Wait. How did you get here?"

"I flew."

"In a plane?" she asked in amazement, as he took the emergency bag from her.

"I don't have wings." He winked at her again and she rolled her eyes. He touched her head. "So who assessed you anyway?"

"There's a camp medic up here. He quickly wrapped my head and we both tackled the more seriously injured." She wobbled a bit and he dropped the bag to catch her.

"Are you okay?"

"Yeah, just dizzy." Her body went limp. "I think the adrenaline that was driving me is easing off."

"Well, let's get you out of here."

"Where's your stretcher?"

"Too much wreckage, and if you're fine I can carry you." George reached down and scooped her up. She wrapped her arms around his neck.

"I feel really dizzy."

"You probably *do* have a concussion, but I'm not a doctor so don't take my word on it."

"Worried I'll sue you for malpractice?" she teased.

"Something like that." George held her close. Her body was trembling, but not in the way it had before. This was different. He didn't like it, he didn't like seeing her in pain.

"If I pass out I want to thank you for coming to get me."

He was going to answer but she moaned and leaned her head against his shoulder. George carried her toward the plane as fast as he could. Once he cleared the debris the crew brought over a stretcher, where they were able to stabilize her.

She let out another moan and then her eyes flew open. "Oh, damn."

"What?" George asked.

"Adam's flying in tomorrow morning. How—?"

"You let me worry about Adam. Don't worry about him. I'll take care of him."

Her eyes filled with tears. "George, I…"

"It's okay."

She smiled up at him. "Thanks for coming to get me."

"You already thanked me." He brushed an errant strand of hair from her eyes.

"I forgot that I did, but thanks anyway."

"Always." George stepped back as they carried her onto the plane. He wasn't sure if she heard him, but it didn't matter. He would tell her again and again.

He was thankful for the chance to be able to tell her anything.

He was thankful she hadn't experienced what he had.

George followed her on the plane, holding onto his bear totem, thanking God, the spirits and anyone who would listen.

He still had to fly them back to Thunder Bay, but that would be easy. He was just glad Samantha was alive.

He wasn't afraid any more.

Things were going to change. He wasn't going to let Samantha go.

It was time to regain control of his life.

It was time to let love in.

CHAPTER FIFTEEN

PAIN WAS THE first thing she experienced when she woke up. Throbbing, horrible pain right behind her eyes.

What the heck happened?

As she pried open her eyes, and her eyelids seemed to scrape her eyeballs like they were made of sandpaper.

White, bright light blinded her for a moment before she got her bearings and then it all came rushing back to her.

The crash.

She tried to sit up but a wave of pain moved through her head, like all this blood had pooled there and was sloshing around. Not to mention that the room was spinning.

"You have a concussion. I wouldn't be trying to, you know, head-bang or anything there, partner."

Samantha looked over at George, who was sitting by her bedside. There were dark circles under his eyes, his face was unshaven, his hair a mess, but he was in street clothing. A T-shirt and jeans.

"How long have I been out?"

"You've been in and out. Your concussion was pretty severe. I'm sure since you're up now they'll get you up and walking."

Samantha winced. "What about Adam?"

"I picked him and Joyce up at the airport. They were understandably worried, but they're in the cafeteria. We haven't been able to prise Adam from your bedside." George nodded toward the cot on the far side of the room. "He only left to get something to eat because I promised to watch you."

Samantha chuckled and then hissed. "Dang, it hurts to laugh."

"Bruised ribs too. That crazy log-camp physician said he triaged you properly—flesh wound, my ass. You could've punctured a lung!"

Samantha rolled her eyes. "Not with bruised

ribs. I suppose I'll be black and blue all over. How's the rest of my team?"

"They're all doing okay. It was touch and go with Mikey, but he'll be fine. His trachea was crushed, but they've repaired it."

Samantha cursed under his breath. "Dammit. Stupid engine. I swear I'm cursed when it comes to engines. First that ambulance in Goderich and now this."

George chuckled. "I think you've had your share of mechanical failures."

She smiled and then she recalled something he'd told her out in the field. Something that made her really sit up and take notice. "You flew."

"I did."

"I thought you couldn't...I thought you wouldn't."

"I can. I do have my pilot's license." His dark eyes twinkled with mischief.

"If I wasn't hooked up to an IV, I'd hit you. You know what I mean."

"As for wouldn't, there are some things worth facing fear for."

She wasn't sure she was hearing him properly. "What're you saying?"

George chuckled. "My fear wasn't that important at the time. It just disappeared with the possibility of a greater fear."

Samantha's heart skipped a beat and the monitor betrayed her. George's lips twitched. "Oh, yes?"

He leaned in and whispered in her ear. "The fear of losing you."

Her eyes pricked with tears. "Me."

"Yes, you." He leaned over and took her hand in his. "Samantha, the thought of losing you, the thought of you dying up there when I could save you was more horrifying to me than my fear of flying."

"Are you saying what I think you're saying?"

George pressed his lips against her knuckles. "I love you Samantha Doxtator. I think I fell in love with that first time we met. I didn't want to admit it. I had been hurt so much I didn't think I could love again. But now I don't want to leave anything unsaid. I love you. I want to be with you and Adam for as long as you'll have me."

The tears streaked down her cheek then, she couldn't control them. "I love you, George. I never thought that I would find love again, or that I would... I was so scared to love again. So scared that it would be taken from me and I didn't want you to be worried about me up in the air. I didn't want you feel any pain if something happened to me."

"Not being with you is worse, Samantha. A life without risks and love is not a life worth living. I know that."

"I love you George. I love you."

George leaned over and kissed her. A chaste kiss but not so chaste that she didn't know exactly what his real intentions were.

Her heart was soaring, it was so full.

The kiss ended sooner than she would've liked, but it was for the best since she was in no position to do anything about it.

"Mom, you're awake!"

Samantha began to cry again when Adam came bounding into the room. There were tears in his eyes as he flung himself into her arms, burying his face against her shoulder.

"Mom, oh, Mom."

"It's okay. I'm okay." She stroked Adam's head.

Joyce followed him in the room, and there were tears in her eyes too as she approached the bed and kissed Samantha on the head. "We thought we were going to lose you, dear."

"Nah," George said. "Never. She's too stubborn for that."

Joyce grinned at George and then smoothed back Samantha's hair. "I see that it's been resolved. Well, I'm glad for it."

"You know?" Samantha asked.

"I maybe old but I'm not senile. I'm happy for you, Samantha. I've been hoping for a long time that you'd find someone." Joyce smiled up at George. "Thank you, George."

"Thank you, Joyce." Samantha was turning

into a blubbering mess. "You know I will love him forever. I'll never forget Cameron."

"I know." Joyce sighed. "Well, I think I'm going to go call Grandpa and then, Adam, we're going to your nana's before I head to the airport tomorrow."

Adam nodded. "Okay, Grandma."

Joyce left the room and it was just the three of them.

"Well?" Adam asked. "Have you asked her yet?"

Samantha looked confused. "Asked me what?"

George tousled Adam's head. "You might as well tell her since you blew the surprise."

Adam grinned. "He wants to marry you."

Samantha's mouth fell open. "You…what?"

"I don't have a ring, but if you'll have me…" He reached round the back of his neck and untied the leather strap, taking off his bear necklace. He placed it around her neck and tied it there. "Bears are for healing. You healed me. I want you to be my wife, Samantha. I want you and Adam in my life for the long haul."

Adam was grinning.

Samantha touched the bear totem. The one his grandmother had carved. Bears were strong, bears were healers, bears were confident.

And she was confident too.

"Yes. Of course I will."

"Yes!" Adam leapt up and did some kind of football dance. "I'm going to tell Grandma." He ran from the room.

George was laughing as he leaned forward and kissed her. "I love you and I have to apologize."

"For what?"

"Well, when you marry me, you marry into my meddling, crazy family and I'm afraid we're going have to spend some Christmases in some pretty damn cold weather."

Samantha chuckled. "Crazy and cold I can handle."

"You say that now."

They kissed again.

Samantha was happy and for the first time in a long time she felt like she deserved to be happy. There were no ghosts haunting her.

There was no more worry and anxiety about what the future might hold.

She had everything she could ever want. Once her injuries were healed she'd go back to her job and work with George. They'd have a good life together, even if it meant they'd have to settle in Nunavut. She didn't care where they lived. As long as she had George and Adam.

There was no more fear. No fear of commitment and no fear of flying.

There was only hope.

And hope overruled fear.

EPILOGUE

One year later

THEY WERE MARRIED on a lookout with the city stretched out before them.

After Samantha got out of the hospital George moved out of his condo and moved in with his new family.

He was awarded a medal from the city for piloting the plane and saving the entire crew of Medic Air Flight 150.

George said it was foolish to award him a medal, but he liked it all the same and Samantha teased him once more about being a dashing hero.

He transferred over to the air side and flew regularly.

It took Samantha a couple of months to get over her concussion. She went through some physio and slept a lot, but by September she was able to fly again.

George helped her through her fear and got her airborne again in no time. They decided to marry on the year's mark of that flight.

The one that had made them realize how foolish they both were being. The day their blinders had come off and they'd realized what they'd had to lose if they didn't follow their hearts.

Adam stood beside George, in a tuxedo that matched his.

Samantha wore an ivory gown. Simple and elegant as she walked down the aisle. Everyone they loved was there.

George's side was full of his family from Cape Recluse. The mothers of two toddlers, one with bright red hair and the other who looked like a mini-George, were trying to control their offspring, but to no avail. On Samantha's side were her mother, sisters, nieces and nephews. As well as Cameron's parents.

George grinned from ear to ear, the wide, infectious smile that made her swoon every time, and she couldn't help but smile back.

They were being married in front of all these people who had supported them, in the city they were going to call home.

Adam stood proudly beside the man he called his father.

When the minister pronounced them man and wife, Samantha threw her arms around George and kissed him, to the cheers of everyone.

Sometimes she'd have to pinch herself, because she would think she didn't deserve to be this happy, but she did.

After they were married George dragged her and Adam over to the memorial, with the wedding photographer in tow.

"What're you doing?"

"I want our wedding photo here. I want our wedding photo to overlook our home."

Samantha kissed him. "I love you, Atavik."

"I love you too."

George yanked Adam into the picture and they stood there together as a family. A family who had finally found their home.

* * * * *

MILLS & BOON®
Large Print Medical

May

PLAYING THE PLAYBOY'S SWEETHEART	Carol Marinelli
UNWRAPPING HER ITALIAN DOC	Carol Marinelli
A DOCTOR BY DAY...	Emily Forbes
TAMED BY THE RENEGADE	Emily Forbes
A LITTLE CHRISTMAS MAGIC	Alison Roberts
CHRISTMAS WITH THE MAVERICK MILLIONAIRE	Scarlet Wilson

June

MIDWIFE'S CHRISTMAS PROPOSAL	Fiona McArthur
MIDWIFE'S MISTLETOE BABY	Fiona McArthur
A BABY ON HER CHRISTMAS LIST	Louisa George
A FAMILY THIS CHRISTMAS	Sue MacKay
FALLING FOR DR DECEMBER	Susanne Hampton
SNOWBOUND WITH THE SURGEON	Annie Claydon

July

HOW TO FIND A MAN IN FIVE DATES	Tina Beckett
BREAKING HER NO-DATING RULE	Amalie Berlin
IT HAPPENED ONE NIGHT SHIFT	Amy Andrews
TAMED BY HER ARMY DOC'S TOUCH	Lucy Ryder
A CHILD TO BIND THEM	Lucy Clark
THE BABY THAT CHANGED HER LIFE	Louisa Heaton